Arry
Eslop

MICHAEL PARFITT

Illustrations by

Rachael Parfitt Hunt

*For my Mother,
the greatest character I have ever known*

CONTENTS

Acknowledgements   1

Preface   3

Part One

The Early Years

1   I Am Born and Given A Name   6

2   The Town Where We Lived   13

3   Our House   22

4   My Mother And The Low Fell Family   31

5   My Father And The Family Holidays   46

6   St. Peter's Grammar School   61

Part Two

Diary of the Early Adult Years

7   The Articled Clerk, 1956 to 1961   81

8   The Holidays, 1956 to 1959   90

9   Football, 1955 to 1957   95

10 The Street Paper Seller, 1955   98

11   The Friend, 1945 to 1989   103

12   The Girlfriend, 1956/57   107

13   The Final Exams, 1961   112

Part Three

Living in London

14   Leaving For London   119

15   Work In London   126

16   The Entrepreneurs   142

Part Four

Assignment in Africa

17   Leaving For Tanganyika   158

18   Mwanza, Tanganyika   169

19   The Office   176

20   The "Ex-Pats" Club   180

21   Safari   193

     About The Author   205

Acknowledgements

Many thanks to the people who have helped me to write this book:

To my wife Anne for not talking so that I could get on with the writing.

To my son Mark who gave me a lot of help with his knowledge of technology, and computer systems in general, and also for his permission to use his photograph of Durham Cathedral and Castle on the cover.

To my daughter Rachael for her illustrations which have helped to bring the story to life.

To Rachael's husband Phil for his expert professional editing.

To my friend Anne Neve-Smith for her helpful and constructive observations on the script.

Also to my friend John Metcalfe for his positive feedback, and for his permission to use his photograph of Michael Jeffery and Harry in Part Two of the book.

Also my thanks to Wikipedia on the Internet which I used to support, and to remind me of, some historical aspects of the narrative in Parts Three and Four of the story.

MICHAEL PARFITT

Finally thank you to Christine Kidney who kindly read Part One of the story and gave me friendly and helpful advice, and encouraged me to continue writing the rest of the book.

Preface

Although this little story is true, and the people described were real people, I have changed their names to protect their identity. Also, the school described in Chapter 6 was the school I attended in my youth. However, I have changed its name and location in order not to disclose its real identity.

The people in the little story were happy people, and the school was a happy school; and I was pleased to grow up in the North East of England at that time, because with the coal mines, ship building and heavy steel industries all going strongly, there was a vibrant atmosphere with the opportunity to work hard and play hard.

Most of the people mentioned in the story are now dead, but if they could be asked if they liked the era in which they lived, I think, despite the hardships, most of them would say they would rather have lived then than at any other time.

Arry Eslop, Part One

The Early Years

My Mam, a beautiful lady with a hat.

1

I AM BORN AND GIVEN A NAME

I was born August 12 1939, just before the start of the Second World War, in the maternity hospital, in a market town with the unlikely name of Bishop Auckland in County Durham in the North East of England.

The hospital was a large old house which had been converted for use as a hospital. There were no funds available at that time, so it was common practice to adapt old houses for such uses.

It was still less than four years since the march for jobs, from Jarrow on Tyneside, to London. With the local people, still haunted by the Jarrow march, and with the memory of unemployment caused by the Great Depression, they were used to making the most of available resources.

I was the fourth of four children with two elder sisters and one elder brother. We were all born within the space of 4½ years, with 1½ years intervals between our birthdays.

As a baby, Mam and I spent most of the time in the kitchen, which, in contrast to my bright and breezy Mam, was the gloomiest room in the whole house. Cradled in her arms she squeezed and pinched me, saying,

"Ooagh, mitchie totches and tinkie poncums,"

with her head thrown back, and an intense expression on her face, like someone with a toffee stuck between their jaws at the back of the mouth.

Although only a young baby, I remember these occasions as peculiar and unusual experiences.

Mam loved me, and my brothers and sisters, with a love that only a Mother knows and understands.

She was a talented and strikingly attractive lady, with a strong will and determination and vivid personality.

In the kitchen was the "delf rack". This was the posh name for the old sideboard which was used for storage of plates. In the bottom half was a cupboard where old clothes were kept. This was home for the cat, who slept there in luxury and comfort. When we lost track of the whereabouts of the cat we heard scratching on the cupboard door and meowing,

"I am in here and I want to come out and go for a walk".

As young children we use words and expressions as if they are the Universal language without questioning their meaning or origin. The use of the words, such as "delf rack", becomes second nature.

The "delf rack" was part of our little World, and we would have thought it unusual if everybody did not have a "delf rack" in their kitchen.

If someone in our family lost something Mam would say,

"It is probably in the kitchen behind a plate on the "delf rack".

My baby's high chair was next to the "delf rack", and I hid bread crusts behind the plates because I didn't want anyone to know I had not eaten them. When they were discovered it was known Arry had left his crusts again.

Later, when I was old enough to share my meals with the rest of the family at the dinner table, I liked to tell them stories while we were eating. These were all very plausible tales and everyone, including the cat, listened attentively.

Without exception, these stories started with the preface,

"There was this man",

followed by an account of "this man's" extraordinary exploits and achievements.

They then concluded with the abjuration,

"He didn't really though". I knew this final caveat was essential having been taught that GOD didn't condone the telling of lies and I wanted to keep HIM as a friend.

My original name was not Arry Eslop. I was baptised "Harry Heslop", but I am now known as Arry Eslop because that is what I have always called myself.

At school there was a French teacher, a Mr Campbell, known to the boys as Big Bill. He was a cynical and sarcastic man. Nevertheless he was something of an enigma, because he was not cruel. In fact he clearly liked the children, and was a talented teacher with a vocation for the work.

The students empathised with him as they also had the Englishman's natural understanding and appreciation of sarcasm.

Big Bill had a large family and usually appeared tired and a bit disappointed with his peregrination through life. He always seemed a little sleepy and, no doubt, his bedtime activity accounted for, not only the regular additions to his family but also his tiredness and pasty complexion.

He was quite a handsome man in his ever present black academic gown, and although English, appropriately for a French teacher, his appearance was that of the typical Frenchman, with his sallow face, and black hair brushed back over his head, helped by a generous application of Brylcream.

He appeared to have a problem with his sinuses, and had a habit of intermittently breathing down his nose and snorting with a sound something like that of the exhaust of a scooter motor bike.

I remember him swinging into the classroom, depositing a pile of exercise books on his desk, turning to look me full in the face and demanding,

"Heslop, *snort, snort*, stand up, *snort, snort*, and tell the   class your name".

Immediately standing to attention at the side of my desk I responded,

"Yes Sir, my name is Arry Eslop".

He snorted down his nose a couple of times, and addressed me, together with the rest of the boys in the class,

"Well done Harry, *snort, snort*, you have illustrated to us, *snort, snort*, how the French people speak, *snort, snort*, when they drop their "H's" This, *snort, snort*, is how I want you all to speak French".

This was at an early stage of our life at secondary school, when in form one, and although my contemporaries had already formed the opinion that Big Bill may not have been completely sane, they had clearly enjoyed this episode, and as impressionable young men, from that day forward, they always called me Arry Eslop.

Big Bill had a good sense of humour and, despite having caused me some embarrassment in front of my fellow students, it was good to see from a trace of a smile on his face that he had been amused by his own wry wit.

Big Bill in his ever-present black academic gown.

2

THE TOWN WHERE WE LIVED

Bishop Auckland is situated in the heart of County Durham, equa-distant from the coastal ports of Newcastle, Sunderland, and Middlesbrough, which are at the mouths of the Tyne, Wear, and Tees respectively. The Tyne defines the North side of the County, with the Tees on the Southern border.

Although the town itself is in a valley, it is at a level higher than the river Wear, which meanders in a gully at the bottom of the valley, before gliding on its way through Durham City, and then onto Sunderland where it flows into the North Sea.

With the advent of the industrial revolution Bishop Auckland grew into a bustling market town with coal mining villages springing up all over the county. When I was young it was a happy place, as the pits were producing lots of coal, and there was a vibrant atmosphere with the local people working hard and playing hard.

The origin of the name "Bishop Auckland" is "Bishop's Oakland".

In the town there is an historic palace where, for many years, the Bishops of Durham have lived. This palace is in a lovely green, natural park, with "oak trees" on the banks of the river Wear. The Bishop's residence is a "palace" because in times gone by the Bishop was also a "Prince". This area is still known as the "Land of the Prince Bishops"

A local legend recalls the story of a wild boar which terrorised the neighbourhood. After it had killed a lot of the local population, the Prince Bishop issued a proclamation offering a substantial reward to anyone who could kill, and bring him the head of the wild boar. The individual who satisfied this challenge would be given as much land as he could ride round in one day.

A man named Jack Pollard was in the locality and he took up the commission and succeeded in catching the wild boar.

When he took the boar's head to show the Prince Bishop he was heartily congratulated and invited to go out on his horse and claim his reward. He complied with this request, but instead of proceeding to ride for a day he simply rode round the Prince Bishop's palace.

This was of course an embarrassment to the Prince Bishop, but he respected Jack Pollard for his astute action and allocated him a substantial chunk of land to the West of Bishop Auckland.

Just under a mile in a Westerly direction from the bottom of our street, across Latherbrush Bridge, there is a pub called Pollard's Inn named after Jack Pollard, a notorious adventurer. In later years, before I first left Bishop Auckland in the early 1960's, I regularly enjoyed Cameron's Strongarm in this local inn.

During the war I have memories of walking along Etherley Lane with Dad, to the old church, and passing German prisoners with identification patches on their shirts. They marched under guard back to the prison camp, and as we passed them Dad greeted them with "Gûten morgen".

At that time Britain was engaged at the height of the war, but where we lived everything seemed tranquil and peaceful.

It was thought that Durham folk lived in the soot and grime of the coal mining industry, but in Bishop Auckland, and in other parts of the area there was countryside as beautiful as any place.

The coal miners had their vegetable allotments on the hill behind the old church, and on Sunday mornings, before going off to the pub, they sat and smoked their pipes and gazed across the Wear valley.

It was good to pass the time of day with the miners and enjoy their humour. One day when I was walking past the allotments down to the river, I passed an old miner and asked if he was keeping well,

"Oh, no man, not so good pet, these past few weeks we have been working in a seam that's so low we were using bent candles".

County Durham also has an impressive industrial history in other respects, with ship building on the Tyne and Wear, iron and steel on Teesside, and a top pedigree in steam trains, with, on September 27, 1825, the World's first public passenger railway, from Shildon to Darlington and then on to Stockton. George Stephenson's "Locomotion No.1" pulled the carriages on this train.

The town had an interesting and unusual Victorian railway station. It had been built, in an extravagant, sprawling manner, in the heyday of the railways. Shaped like a large triangle, it enabled a whole train to turn round without detaching the engine.

A train from Darlington to Crook Town, arrived at the platform forming one side of the triangle, and then pulled out of the station, but instead of continuing to Crook, reversed through the Crook to Durham City platform, and then moved forward onto the Durham City to Darlington track. In this way the train had completed a turn, and was now ready to make the return journey to Darlington, and the manoeuvre had been accomplished without the need to transfer the engine to the other end of the train.

It is surprising this technique was not adopted more generally in the railway system. However this may have been because of the large area of land occupied by a triangular shaped station.

Sadly, with the decline of regional railways, this fascinating monster of a station, was recently pulled down, and partly replaced by a supermarket with a large car park.

Up to the 1950's this network of rail track was

well used by both passenger and freight traffic. It was also an important route for main line trains when they were diverted to avoid the Sunday engineering work on the direct railway between Darlington and Durham City.

My brother Trevor and I were both steam rail enthusiasts, and it was a special day when, from our dining room window, we saw the smoke from an express snaking its way through the town.

We shouted,

"Diversion!"

and ran down the hill to take up our usual position on a wall, close to a bend in the track, to watch these elegant trains go by.

It was exciting to see majestic engines, like "Mallard" and "Ocean Swell", hauling long trains of coaches, and slowly winding their way through the town, with sleepy passengers wondering what they had done wrong to deserve this interminable mystery tour.

The Co-operative Society (Co-op) had by far the largest store in the town. It sold everything from a packet of sugar to a garden spade. It is owned by its members who are the store's customers, and having no shareholders, the profits are distributed to the members in the form of dividends. The local people, including my mother, did their shopping there and found the dividends helpful.

The Co-op had a remarkable cash handling system. When the customer paid, the cash, together with a note of the price of the goods, was placed in a small metal tub attached to a pulley. Then the salesperson, with a downward pull of a cord, sent the tub flying across the store on a rope, which was something like a taut clothes' line, to a kiosk where there was a central cashier. There was a network of these "clothes' lines" all around the store. The cashier took the cash, and placed the change in the tub, before firing it back to the sales counter.

No doubt this was a sophisticated method of internal cash control, and it seemed an impressive system particularly for young children as they were fascinated with the little metal tubs flashing around the store.

The Co-op was a large local industry in its own right, with their milk bottling factory next to the railway station, and bakery, and livestock slaughter house, also in that vicinity.

The milk was delivered to the bottling plant

from the station, where it had arrived on the "milk train" which was usually hauled by a main line engine; an additional interest for the local train spotting enthusiasts.

Close to the bakery and milk depot, there were stables for the horses which were used for the delivery of the bread and milk to the houses of the Co-op's many customers.

These were fine big horses, similar to the drayhorses that were used to deliver the beer. They were also clever animals.

The milkman, who delivered to our street, seemed to be completely detached from his horse and wagon, and simply walked backwards and forwards from the wagon, picking up milk bottles and placing them on the door steps. The horse knew where to stop at the customers' houses, and if she just had the physical ability to pick up a bottle she could have completed the round by herself with no assistance whatsoever from the milkman.

The town was blessed with an exceptionally large number of pubs. There were numerous drinking houses in Newgate Street (the town's main street), and many more in the side streets and alleys, which ran off the main street. Bondgate, in particular was well endowed, where at one point there were three pubs all joined together on one side of the road, and two more immediately opposite. There were also about half a dozen hostelries, including working men's clubs, in the market place.

The town's famous football club, Bishop Auckland AFC, which has a proud history and tradition, had its home at the Kingsway ground.

3

OUR HOUSE

A few days before Christmas 1942, my brother Trevor and I stood in our bedroom and looked out of the window with excited anticipation as snow was beginning to fall. It had been a very cold day, and the sky heavy with dark grey cloud.

As it was early evening, the street lamp-man walked up the road with the long pole he used to light the gas lamps, and lit the one on the corner at the end of the street outside our bedroom window. In the warm, orangey, yellow glow of the gas lamp large snowflakes were blowing around agitated by the angry wind.

We joyfully looked forward to snow in the morning, and stood there with bare feet frozen to the lino on the bedroom floor without feeling the cold.

Our house was on the highest ground in the town at the top of Clarence Bank and the bedroom, exposed to the harsh weather, was very cold.

The local people, understandably, insist the North East is at least two top coats colder than London. That day, with the wind blowing in off the North Sea, it was cold enough to freeze the balls off a brass monkey.

We breathed on the frozen window to help remove the frost and give a better view of the snow which was now falling heavily.

Then the cat came into the bedroom, and jumped up onto the window sill beside where we were standing, to share our view. She had been hiding in her cupboard, frightened by the howling wind; but now she sensed the calmness, created by the blanket of snow on the ground, and the drifts sealing the gaps in the windows and doors.

We could see the snow had frozen to the sides of the buildings and trees, helping to complete a magic picture of peace and tranquillity. The snow had muffled the noises caused by the wind, but it was still blowing hard, sending the flakes up and down and in all directions, and this fascinated the delighted cat.

Trevor and I were happy, as the day before we had returned home from the local nursery. However, our return was not in auspicious circumstances.

The nursery was a prefabricated building which had been hastily erected in a corner of the recreation ground at the foot of the steep hill in front of our house. This nursery was for young children whose parents needed support because of difficulties encountered due to the war.

We had been sent to live at the nursery for a few days as Mam needed a break from bringing up four young children.

As we were unhappy there; after the first night, Trevor told me we were going to escape. He was in charge of the breakout, and I his willing lieutenant. When no one was looking, Trevor climbed over the perimeter fence and pulled me after him.

We made our way through the rec and out of the gate at the foot of the bank, and up the steep hill back to the front door of our house.

Mam heard our knocking and opened the door.

Seeing us standing there like two forlorn little beggars, she exclaimed,

"Oh, what have you done? What has happened?"

A nurse who had followed replied,

"I saw them climbing over the nursery fence, and came after them to see where they would go".

When asked why we had done this, Trevor explained,

"We didn't like it there. There was only had one 'cloe' on the bed".

Feeling better now we were back in our own bedroom, we looked forward to a happy Christmas the next week.

It was soon time for bed, and we jumped in, and breathed under the blankets to create warmth.

It had been an eventful day. Maureen had thought her elder sister Pat had taken the last rock bun off the plate, and as Dad and Mam thought Maureen was right, Pat was upset, and insisted that she hadn't eaten it.

Before we went to sleep, we heard our sisters coming up the stairs, and as they passed our bedroom, Pat telling herself,

"Anyway GOD knows I didn't eat the rock bun!"

Pat and Maureen's bedrooms were at the front of the house; Pat's was above the downstairs hallway, with a window above the front door. Maureen's was next to Pat's, with a similar window looking out in the same direction.

Clarence Street was a road of solid, stone built, Victorian houses facing onto the street, but the end houses had fronts facing away from the terrace, like two book-ends.

All the houses had Georgian-style sash bedroom windows, and large bay windows downstairs.

Dad and Mam's bedroom was on the corner, above the dining room, and had one window at the front with a panoramic view over the town to the golf course on the High Plains. There was another window in their room at the side, and this one looked out to the street lamp.

The dining room was bright and cheerful with two bay windows. It had a bright and airy feel about it, and was the most pleasant room in the whole house. Strangely, although it was used for Christmas, it was rarely in service at any other time of the year.

The bathroom upstairs appeared to have been added to the house as an after-thought. It seemed to be sticking out of the house side, and was situated above the out-houses in the back yard.

One of the out-houses was a toilet, and there were two other out-houses used for the storage of coal.

The house also boasted two fine dry cellars, one with its own open fire, where there was also a tub and a mangle which Mam used for the laundry, before hanging the clothes out in the back lane to dry.

The open fireplace was never used, except on the occasion of my twenty-first birthday when my parents were away on holiday. On that day the whole house was thrown open, and we had a large log fire in that cellar which luckily didn't send the house up in flames.

Health and Safety inspectors were conspicuous by their absence in those days. If one had visited our home, and had enjoyed writing long reports, he would have had a field day.

There were gas fires in the bedrooms which appeared to be a hundred years old. Trevor and I had a fire lighting technique which involved turning on the gas and then taking refuge behind the bed, before throwing a match at the fire, causing an explosion as the flames were ignited. Throwing the match was a sensation a bit like tossing a hand grenade.

In addition to the toilet in the outhouse, there was also one in the peculiarly attached bathroom. As there was no cash available for the purchase of toilet roles, old newspapers were recycled for this purpose. They were torn into square packs and placed behind the cistern pipe at the back of the toilet. Everyone went around with black bums, with the printers' ink deposited on their backsides.

There was no fridge, but the cellars were ideal for cool storage. After breakfast the pack of bacon was thrown down the cellar stairs, where it was kept for future use. Retrieving the bacon for the next breakfast involved a precarious excursion down the steep cellar stairs.

The traders, making their door to door deliveries of various produce, like bread and milk, were an absorbing feature of daily life.

Mam bought from a bloke who came up the street with his horse and cart, calling,

"Calorerrin!"

I never knew what this meant but, as he sold fish, I assumed that he traded in "herring", and Calor was the port where the fish was landed. However to this day I have never heard of a port named Calor.

I now know from reference to the Oxford English dictionary that "caller" (pronounced with a hard "a") is a Scottish word meaning "fresh".

The "New Geordie Dictionary" also mentions,

"Caller. Fresh. Caller herrin – a well known street cry".

The man who sold fish in our street may have been from one of the fishing ports near the mouth of the Tyne, such as North Shields, and his Geordie dialect may have pronounced "caller" as "calor".

Mam, who was from Low Fell in Gateshead, was probably familiar with this street cry, and may have had no difficulty in understanding the man.

"Caller herrin" – *a well-known street cry.*

4

MY MOTHER AND THE LOWFELL FAMILY

My Mam wore a hat. In fact I don't remember seeing her outside of the house without a hat on her head.

She hadn't many hats, four at the most; perhaps one for each season of the year. They were looked after very carefully, and she always looked smart and attractive.

They were charming hats, and would have been the envy of the top film stars of the day.

At all times of my life, I remember Mam as a beautiful lady with a hat.

At a later time, when my family was living in Surrey, and Mam and Dad came to spend holidays with us, we would meet at King's Cross station, and I knew I couldn't miss them, so long as I watched out for a hat getting off the train.

In earlier years Mam and Dad loved the family holidays, and as children we looked forward to them. They will never be forgotten for as long as we live. However, when we had grown up and gone our own ways it was not possible for us to get together for these occasions.

My children were born overseas, and as we lived abroad for the first years of their lives Mam and Dad saw very little of them at that time. When we returned to live in the UK it was lovely when they had the opportunity to visit us and spend time with their grandchildren. I know these were special times for them.

Originally they came together, but as time went by the journey became too difficult for Dad because of his failing health, and these visits became impossible for a while, before the sad time of Dad's death.

With Mam continuing to live in the North East as a widow, the opportunity to get away to visit for a holiday became even more important. This was so evident from her smile when we first saw each other, as the hat arrived on the train at the station.

We lived in Surrey next to the North Downs,

and Mam enjoyed the beautiful views in these open spaces.

One time when Mam was staying at our house on holiday, our Daughter, Rachael, woke up in the morning to find her hamster had escaped from its cage. Mam saw us searching for something, and mentioned,

"Oh, I was woken during the night when a little furry thing walked over my face, so I picked it up, put it out on the landing, closed the bedroom door, and went back to sleep again".

We eventually found the hamster elsewhere in the house, looking pleased with its nocturnal exploration.

Mam loved animals, and talked to our cat, Bisto, (she was called Bisto because she went around with her nose in the air, like she was sniffing the gravy freshly poured over the Sunday roast) as though the cat was human, and it responded accordingly.

Mam was a good impersonator and mimic, and when she portrayed animals she gave them human characteristics.

One day I came downstairs and did nothing more than say "hello" to the cat, but it looked me straight in the eye, and yawned with a long yawn, as though to say,

"You are unbelievably boring, you great big silly Billy".

As time went by, and Mam became frail with advancing age, it was a privilege to drive with her up to the North Downs. I took a wheel chair in the car boot so we were able to have an outing in the fresh air. As I wheeled her along in the chair, I noticed that, despite her failing hearing, she could hear me much better when I was walking behind her than when we talked face to face. She generally found it difficult to hear me because my voice does not carry. Fortunately, my wife has a more crisp North East dialect which Mam could hear very well.

Mam was a strong character who expressed her point of view in no uncertain manner in order to look after the family.

Her Father, Grandpa Milburn was also a strong character and had built up a coal delivery business, which with careful management of the profits had protected his family from the hard times experienced by many of the local population, and had provided for a good education for his children.

Mam herself had graduated from the London Royal Academy of Music, and was a first rate classical pianist. When we wrote to her we always recognised the qualification with her address as "Mrs O A Heslop LRAM, ARCM".

The great luxury in our house was the grand piano in the lounge. It was treated with respect, being regularly professionally tuned.

Some of us in the family tended to take this music for granted, but, thinking back, it must have been an exceptional experience for the people walking past the house to hear this performed with such perfection, particularly on a summer's day when it could be heard clearly through the open windows.

Mam was careful, and a good manager of the housekeeping money, because, like her Father, she was determined her children would be encouraged to complete a worthwhile education. Her money management was remarkable and impressive. She never wasted a penny.

One day, when I was just about five years old, her economic ways proved embarrassing for me. We had woken up that morning to find deep snow on the ground, and as I didn't have wellington boots (probably because I would soon grow out of them, and as I was the youngest of the children, there was no one to pass boots down to), she pulled a pair of long socks over the outside of my shoes, and sent me off to school dressed in this fashion. I was told to ask the teacher to dry the socks on the radiator, and as the teacher, a Miss Jones, could see I was shy about my attire, she was kind to me, and dried the socks as Mam had requested.

Although only five at the time, I appreciated that Miss Jones was a beautiful young lady teacher. I was full of admiration, and the first time I saw her I fell in love. I am sure it was my high regard for her that made my first year at school a happy one.

Mam's money management skills were exceptionally good, for example, she didn't buy brand names of food like Whiskas, as this she considered an extravagance. Instead of this, the cat was fed on tripe bought from Titch Pinchitter, the local fishmonger, who sold tripe as a sideline.

Mr. Pinchitter was a tight arsed, tall, skinny man, with a globule of snot always just about to drip from the end of his beaky nose. Over the years he had developed an appearance similar to the wet fish which he sold.

The tripe Mam bought at his shop was blood red and messy, but our cat thought it delicious. Mr Pinchitter wrapped it in old newspaper, and it was stored like this, on the stone floor, at the bottom of the cellar stairs in our house to keep it cool, until it was fed to the cat over the course of a few meals.

Mr. Pinchitter was one of the local star turns. He was noted for his bargaining ability, and would haggle over a halfpenny.

He had adopted his nickname "Titch", as his official title, because he didn't like "Hokey", the real name given him by his parents.

Another one of Mam's notable economies was the use of her little finger to scrape the inside of the shell, to ensure she used the last drop of the white of an egg when she was cooking.

There were also memorable occasions when a Miss Elsie Benderear called to trade her packet of sugar for a few ounces of Mam's tea. This barter arrangement was conducted at great length in our dining room, as a major covert black market transaction, during the war time food rationing.

The rest of the family waited in trepidation when they heard this lady approaching the front door, because the meeting always resulted in three hours tittle-tattle, with little prospect of escape in order to close up the house and go to bed.

Miss Benderear was a thin woman, with the appearance of one living on tea, and nothing else. She had a pasty face relieved only by the rouge applied to her cheeks. She wore an old cloth hat which matched her suit, both of which had at one time been bright red, but had worn down to a pale dusty pink with long exposure to the elements. She had a theatrical appearance, and the colour of her clothes reminded me of the stage curtains at one of the old local cinemas which were the same dusty pink.

Mam was born and bred in Low fell, Gateshead, on the Durham side of the river Tyne.

She was one of a large family of characters, all of whom had vivid personalities.

Miss Benderear was a thin woman, with the appearance of one living on tea, and nothing else.

Her Father, Grandpa Milburn was an elegant gentleman, with white hair. He was always immaculately turned out in a smart tweed suit with a gold watch on a fob in the waistband of his breeches.

He was loved and respected by the whole family, and also by the people of Low Fell.

I remember him as a Godfather figure, recognised as a wise man, whose encouragement and guidance benefited everyone.

He took a keen interest in sport, particularly football and horse racing.

Just before he died he forecast the winners of the Derby and the Grand National, and told us Newcastle United would win the FA Cup. All these predictions proved to be correct; Newcastle won the cup, and I think it was Dante that won the Derby, but I can't remember the winner of the Grand National that year.

Grandpa was a good man who lived a very worthwhile life. Although he had a high regard for the beliefs of others, he himself only went to church twice during his lifetime; to be baptised, and then to be married. His final attendance was at his funeral, when we all turned up as part of a large crowd to pay our last respects.

New Year was big in Grandpa's house, as also a major celebration in all of Tyneside, where it was recognised very much as in Scotland. There was a difference in those days as it was not a Bank Holiday in England, unlike Scotland. This had little influence in Newcastle, where the banks' doors were left just slightly ajar, as a token recognition of being "open", but nobody called in to do business.

As children we went to the New Year's Day party. All the families turned up; parents, uncles, aunts, and cousins.

Aunty Norah still lived at the family home, and served lovely homemade apple pies, cakes, sandwiches, savoury meats and fish, and mince pies.

I sat next to Uncle Eddie, and he ensured all the children were kept well served; continually passing us the plates with what he knew was our favourite food.

Everyone was contented and happy at these parties.

After the meal our uncles had drinks, and played dominoes with us.

We liked to hear them talking in their distinctive, rich, Newcastle dialect, which had a sing-song sound, very different from the rather flat tone we knew at home in central County Durham.

I sometimes wonder if Uncle Eddie, and some of the others, may have been missing their night out at the pub, but that didn't seem the case at the time.

Uncle Eddie was a craftsman and had hand carved the beautiful solid oak dining room sideboard and table. He was also a skilful artist with examples of his paintings hanging in the house.

His talents earned plenty of money, but as soon as he received it, he spent it. When asked why he never had any money, he replied, with the Newcastle rolling of the "R's" in the throat at the back of the tongue,

"Well man, money's made rr-ound to go a-rr-ound".

The family were all larger than life, with humour, and big personalities, particularly Aunty Millie with her dark glasses and sombre clothes, contrasting with her bright facial expressions. She had a quick mind and liked to laugh when she saw the funny side of the various individual family traits.

I don't recall ever meeting Grandma Milburn, but I remember Mam telling me how Aunty Norah had nursed her with loving care through a long illness, before she finally died, which may have been at a time before I was born.

Low Fell was aptly named because "fell" in Geordie means "hill", and the whole area is one big hill falling from east to west.

At the end of these parties we walked down the steep hill to the Cannon public house, to catch the last OK bus service back to Bishop Auckland.

The OK bus ran a direct service through Pity Me and Chester-le-Street, whereas the other service (the Northern) called at the Durham City bus station, thus taking considerably longer, as it had to negotiate the narrow streets of this famous historic town.

We knew we were making our way through the outskirts of Low Fell, when we saw the end of the tram lines from Newcastle; and when, there during the war, we could see the last of the barrage balloons which were used to protect the important shipbuilding industry on the Tyne and the Wear from the enemy's low flying aircraft.

My Dad, who had a system which selected horses on a pre-determined track record basis.

5

MY FATHER AND THE FAMILY HOLIDAYS

I know my Dad was born in Leatherhead in Surrey, but I am not too sure how he came to live in Bishop Auckland.

My Sister, Maureen, told me recently that Dad met Mam on an OK bus going from Bishop Auckland to Newcastle. I don't know how he came to be on that bus, but over the years we gleaned snippets of information, which when pieced together give a reasonable account of where he was at various times.

He ran away from school when he was sixteen years old, and joined the army.

There were aspects of school life which he found disagreeable, and eventually when subjected to the school's swimming teaching technique, he decided to leave.

He did learn to swim, but could have just as easily drowned, after being thrown into the pool by the "sports" teacher, who thought this "make or break" approach to learning very efficient.

Leaving the school and joining the army proved to be "out of the frying pan, into the fire", as he was immediately sent off to France, to participate in the First World War, where he specialised as a Morse code signaller. This entailed standing on the highest ground, with signalling flags, where he was an enticing target for pot shots from the enemy.

Clearly he survived this traumatic episode in his life; otherwise he would not have met Mam on the OK bus.

It was not until after Dad's death that I discovered I was a trustee for a Mr. Neville Appleton, who was Dad's son from his first marriage. During his lifetime, for some unknown reason, we were never told about Dad's first wife, but we now know that she died before he met Mam; and our half brother Neville, had adopted his Mother's maiden name.

It transpired that Neville had immigrated to the USA, where he had worked in Virginia as a coal mining engineer.

Although I have never met Neville, I got to know him quite well, as the small trust involved a considerable volume of correspondence and telephone calls. He still had a County Durham dialect, and, like me, is a keen supporter of Sunderland football club. He also liked a pint of Young's Special beer, when he had lived for a while in the London area.

Dad's background was always something of a mystery, particularly on his Father's side, as he was never mentioned. We gathered that he worked in London as a solicitor, and it seems his Father may have separated from his wife, before Dad moved to the North East of England.

Dad, himself, sometimes indicated that he would have been happy to have followed in his Father's profession, and studied to be a solicitor, but this was not to be. Instead it appears that when he first arrived in the North East, he worked as some kind of chemist in the coal mining industry.

Later on he studied insurance and passed the exams to qualify, before starting his own business as an incorporated insurance broker.

He then proceeded to develop the business which was of high quality, and very well respected in the industry, and by the general public. It produced the income which provided for the welfare of our family.

Dad also took up a correspondence course in languages, specialising in French, and graduated as a Fellow of the Institute of Linguists.

He had a lot of interests. Like Grandpa Milburn he loved horse racing and football; but he and Mam also enjoyed tennis, and they both liked walking in the beautiful local countryside.

Dad had a professional approach to horse racing. There was a bookcase in our dining room which he had filled with the fat, brown backed, Sporting Chronicle Handicap books.

He carefully studied the racing form, and had a system which selected horses on a pre-determined track record basis. His credit account arrangement with the leading book-makers included an agreement for them to run the system on his behalf. It was quite successful, as after a time this agreement was cancelled by William Hill, Wanless & Pallister, Corals, and Ladbrokes. Dad told me how the system worked, but I was sworn to secrecy, and to this day have never told anyone the formula.

When on holiday in Devon, Dad and Mam both enjoyed attending the National Hunt meetings at Newton Abbot, and at the Devon and Exeter race course.

Dad was a supporter of Sunderland football club. Mam and the Low Fell family could never understand this, because they, of course being from Low Fell, were supporters of Newcastle United. However, it is quite logical, because Sunderland is the biggest club in County Durham, and we lived in the heart of the county; whereas Newcastle lies on the north side of the Tyne in Northumberland.

It is also true to mention that, in the years before the start of the Second World War, Sunderland was probably the greatest football club in the World, when they were known as

"The team of all the talents".

However, it has to be said that they have been rubbish for most of my life.

Sunderland supporters spend a lot of time talking about statistics, because in recent years we have rarely had a football team worth discussing.

There are questions like,

"Last season, which was the worst team that

played in front of the biggest crowd?"

"Sunderland, with a gate of 48,000 all seated at the Stadium of Light."

Dad's Mother had also moved to the North East. She was a gentle and kind old lady with grey hair, who always had a tin of boiled sweets in the cupboard in her lounge. When I was little she gave me a sweet each time I visited her cosy, but dark house, where she lived alone. The house was in a long terraced street on a hill, with well built, but drab and monotonous buildings.

Often when I visited Grandma Heslop, Dad's sister, Aunty Jean would be there with a board on her knees for the cards with which she played patience.

Aunty Jean worked as a nurse at the hospital. She had a simple outlook on life, and although she appeared to have no ambition, she was dedicated to her nursing vocation, and was respected for the loving care she gave to the patients.

She lived by herself in a frugal, very old cottage, and never seemed at all interested in life's creature comforts.

Aunty Jean was a happy human being in her own way, particularly when she called to see us at Christmas, with her little, carefully wrapped presents for the children.

Dad had another sister, Aunt Cecelia, who had continued to live in London. I saw her only once, when she came to see us, accompanied by her poodle dog. We had the impression that she was quite eccentric, but that may not have been so. At that time we thought any old lady from London was unusual.

Unlike Mam's family, Dad didn't seem all that close to his Sisters, but, thinking back that may well have been a mistaken impression.

One day he answered the telephone in the hall, at the foot of the stairs, and I could see he was upset with the news. In fact it was the only time I ever saw him cry —— Aunty Jean had died!

Mam put her arm round his shoulder to comfort him. It was a picture that told they had always supported each other, and were a strong unit, which had helped them to battle through some of the difficult times they had experienced together.

I drove them to the hospital to see Aunty Jean where she had passed away. She had been a legend in that hospital, and the nurses, who had cared for her at the end, were sad and shocked.

When we came out to the car to make our way back home, I saw that Dad had forgotten his walking stick, so I went back to the ward to collect it. Entering the room where Aunty Jean was lying, I saw the walking stick standing in a corner, but at the same time noticed a little smile on Aunty Jean's face. I bent over and kissed the side of her head, and said a little prayer to myself, asking God to look after her.

When I arrived back at the car, I told Dad that Aunty Jean was happy now, because I had seen this smile. I think this helped to console him, because he had strong faith, and believed in life after death. At that moment my belief was in tune with his.

This was one of the saddest times, but over the years there were many happy events.

Occasionally, as a special treat, Dad took Trevor and me to Roker Park to watch Sunderland play, where, in the post war years, we were part of a crowd which was regularly in excess of 60,000.

There was always a great atmosphere in the ground, and in those days we saw players like

Trevor Ford and Len Shackleton.

Trevor Ford was a bustling centre forward with a powerful shot.

One game against Stoke City he hit the ball so hard, it smashed the City goalkeeper (a man called Herod) full in the face, and knocked him out cold. It took the trainer a full five minutes to revive him before he was carried off the field. It was only then that the goalkeeper learned that he had saved the shot, as, after hitting his face, the ball had gone up and bounced on the crossbar, before going behind the goal, and out of play.

In those days there was no problem in dispersing the large Roker Park crowds after the game. Just before the final whistle, scores of trams formed a long queue outside of the ground, and when the supporters came surging out, they simply jumped on the nearest tram, and were soon transported back to the centre of Sunderland.

Dad would then take us for afternoon tea at one of the town's restaurants, before catching the train back to Bishop Auckland.

The family holiday was the big event of the year. We all looked forward to them, and it seemed that in some respects, Dad lived for these annual breaks. He loved Devon, and we had some great holidays in Torquay, Babbacombe, and Dawlish.

The long journeys by steam train were big adventures, and an important part of the whole holiday. My interest in steam engines increased each day leading up to the holiday.

The daily milk train waited under the footbridge at Bishop Auckland station, and I stood on the bridge, and watched it building up steam, before shunting the carriages into the siding where the milk was collected. The driver sometimes deliberately caused the engine's wheels to spin to show off the locomotive's power. This fascinating picture of railway activity helped us to anticipate the excitement of travel on the main line trains.

The smell of the smoke and the steam gave a lasting, nostalgic memory of those great days on Britain's railways.

Preparing for the holiday was a big job for Mam, because she packed a large trunk of clothes which was sent "luggage in advance". Mam, like most women, had no concept of time, but somehow the trunk was ready when the railway people came to collect it.

When the big day arrived, we took the

connecting train from Bishop Auckland to Darlington, before catching the express to London.

As the local train started to pull out of the station at the start of our journey, Dad's whole body visibly relaxed into the back of the carriage seat, as he breathed a sigh of relief, knowing that the holiday had now started.

Standing on Darlington station waiting for the express to arrive from Newcastle, Trevor and I speculated about the name of the locomotive that would be pulling our train on the London leg of the journey. As this part of the trip usually took about five and a half hours, it was normal for us to have an overnight reservation at a London hotel, before continuing the journey to Devon the next day.

Dad liked to check the train's speed on the Darlington to York stretch of the railway, which was good straight track. The 42 miles were covered in 42 minutes, and this average 60 mph was good going. We checked the speed with the second hand of Dad's watch, as we timed the train between the little white, quarter miles, marker posts at the side of the track.

Following our overnight stop in London, we made our way to Paddington station to start the onward journey to Devon.

For this part of the trip we travelled on the appropriately named Great Western Railway. It was truly a great railway, with the lovely chocolate and cream painted carriages, and the green engines, with the distinctive gold band around the rim of the smoke funnel.

This railway's employees took a pride in their jobs, and the company for which they worked.

I remember one year we were standing ankle deep in water on Paddington station, but we were still in good spirits, and said it should have been called Paddlington station. This must have been at the time of the great floods in the summer of 1952.

In the earlier post war period it seemed everyone wanted to go on holiday after the years of austerity, and we were all packed in the train's corridors like sardines in a can. It must have been claustrophobic for the adults, but for us children it was all part of the big adventure.

One year when we were on holiday in Dawlish, I happily joined a mile long queue on the beach, for a bar of Wall's ice cream. It was a long time since anyone had tasted an ice cream, in view of the war time food rationing.

The spectacular train ride was at its best along the South Devon coast near Dawlish, where the train seemed to be travelling through the sea, as the track was so close to the water's edge. It was lovely to see the waves crashing on the rocks and beaches, as the train wound its way along the coastline.

Our favourite destination was the Stratford Hotel, owned by Mr. Briton. This was in Wellswood, which is in between Torquay and Babbacombe.

To call the establishment an "hotel" was perhaps an overstatement, but it was clean and comfortable, with good wholesome food. It may have lacked a woman's touch, because Mr. Briton was a widower, and he ran his hotel in a kind of military fashion. The meals, announced by the sound of a gong in the front hallway, were always served dead on time, and we felt quite guilty if we were the ones who turned up a few seconds late.

The toilets and bathrooms were on the landings, at the top of each flight of stairs, between the four floors in the building. It was often a relief to gain access to the toilets, particularly just after breakfast, when they tended to be in most demand.

Nevertheless, we were always made very welcome, and were happy there, going back year after year, as did most of the other guests; and Mr. Briton became a good friend.

I remember long hot, sunny, summers, rarely interrupted with rain and bad weather.

The train journey home was another exciting experience, but then we were all more subdued. We sat in the train with sun tanned faces, as brown as berries.

Following another memorable holiday, and after the long day, we were often cheered up by the late Summer North East of England lovely sunset, when we were on the little steam train from Darlington back to Bishop Auckland.

*The little steam train that ran from
Darlington to Bishop Auckland.*

6

ST. PETER'S GRAMMAR SCHOOL

I was first introduced to St. Peter's about one year before I started to attend as a student.

Trevor had commenced as a new pupil, and one day he forgot his lunch-time sandwiches. Mam's solution to this problem was to ask me to deliver the sandwiches, so she gave me the money for the ten mile fare to Durham City, and told me to catch the next bus.

As I was only ten years old at the time, I was given detailed instructions about where to get off the bus, and how to make my way to the school, which was on the outskirts of the city.

After leaving the bus, I walked for a mile along a pleasant residential road, before turning into a long drive which led up to the school. The drive ran through a wooded area before breaking out into a large open space. At this point I saw the school for the first time.

It was a lovely big mansion dating back to the early Victorian era. Before being converted for use as the school, it had for many years been the home of a family of a celebrated local dignitary.

The beautiful stone built building had been preserved intact, as had the solidly structured stables, which were in a big yard not far from the main building, and converted for use as the school's dining room.

It stood in spacious grounds, part of which were used for the remarkable number of six separate football pitches. As the school only had about 180 pupils, this was indeed an extraordinary number of football pitches.

Trevor was still in form one where the classroom was on the ground floor on the corner of the building, first encountered on the approach, and next to the drive. I met one of the teachers when I went in, and asked where I would find Trevor, and he kindly showed me into the classroom, where Big Bill happened to be taking the lesson.

I explained the purpose of my visit, and Big Bill called out to Trevor,

"Heslop, I gather you have forgotten your

lunch today, *snort, snort*, and I would like you, *snort, snort*, to thank this young man, *snort, snort*, for coming all this way, *snort, snort*, to deliver it to you.

The other boys in the class were clearly delighted to have my visit as a diversion from the normal course of the lesson, but I think it was a source of some embarrassment for Trevor.

About a year later my parents and I were greatly relieved when we learned that I had passed the "eleven-plus" tests, which meant that I could also attend the school.

Mam took me off to Durham, where there was a shop that sold the school uniform. This was a light blue blazer and cap, both with the school badge and motto, "Fortes in fide". I didn't wear this uniform again until the first day of the Autumn term, after the long Summer holiday.

There was a typical cross section of students at the school, and although many could have been categorised as rogues, I think the large majority were proud of the school, and would not have liked the uniform to have been brought into disrepute.

The teachers and the boys both realised we

were lucky to have this school in a lovely setting, for such a small number of pupils.

The head master, Father Cunningham (Foxy) encouraged pride in the establishment, and his leadership influenced the teachers and boys in this respect. There was a good atmosphere, and generally speaking we were all happy.

The Country was still struggling to get back to some kind of normality after the war years, and there was a severe shortage of teachers. I know our form took French as our modern foreign language for the first two years, and then had to switch to Spanish for the following years, because the timetable couldn't accommodate a continuation of French teaching. This resulted in most of us leaving school with a confused knowledge of not much of either language.

However, Big Bill's remarkable teaching technique enabled us to pass "O" level Spanish, and he probably could have got us through French as well, if that had been required.

When he was teaching French he advised us to learn the story, "A bird of paradise". This is a tale of a bird which escapes from its cage, and goes to amuse itself in the fields and the woods. It then gets lost, and becomes very hungry, but luckily, when it has almost starved to death, it finds a pile of grain. The moral of the story is, "Il ne faut jamais se laissez aller au désespoir" (Never despair). It includes idiomatic French phrases, and Big Bill advised us to lift selected parts of the story, and drop them into our written examination, because there was always a question like "Write a short essay about a day's outing in the countryside", and the answer could accommodate passages from the story.

When we switched to Spanish we were told to learn something about, "Quando yo era joven pasado mis vacaciones en el campo con mis tios", and use it in the GCE "O" level exam in the same manner.

The headmaster, Father Cunningham (Foxy),
encouraged pride in the establishment.

Father Murray (Pop Murray) was the Latin teacher. He was a jovial, stocky man with a fat tummy; and could have made a good Friar Tuck alongside Robin Hood.

He was happy at the school, but had no gift, or aptitude for teaching. In fact if he had switched from teaching Latin to Chinese half way through a lesson, we wouldn't have noticed any difference.

He smoked a lot of cigarettes as he felt they gave him relief from the pain inflicted by his stomach ulcer.

He would come bouncing into the classroom with a cigarette in his hand, and say,

"Come on lads, now what is it?"

Then taking a huge drag of the fag, so the end shone out bright red, and then inhaling deeply, he would continue,

"In with the ab".

When this brought no result he went on

"In with the abla".

At this point we responded with,

"Ablative Father".

He was then quite pleased with the progress, and proceeded to change the subject to football. The rest of the lesson would be happily spent picking the teams for the next house matches.

Needless to say Latin always remained a complete mystery to me, and most of the other boys.

Like Trevor and me, there were a number of boys attending the school from the same families. The Skillit family was one such example.

The Skillit brothers had no natural ability for languages anyway, but they were very good at physics and chemistry. Although brothers they were very different from each other in some ways. The elder brother, Skull Skillit, was quite aggressive, and had a cruel streak. He was a leader in exercising the school's initiation tradition, where one aspect was throwing new boys into the nettles behind the bicycle sheds.

On the other hand his brother Tim was a rather plump, mild, young fellow who went around humming romantic pop tunes to himself.

They were very enthusiastic about their chemistry studies and tried experiments at home.

One of these was to use the bathroom scales both before, and after a big pooh. When the second weighing indicated no loss of weight, they were puzzled, and disappointed with the failure of the experiment.

Another effort involved directing a fart at a lighted candle. In this event they were delighted when the gas caused the candle flame to glow and flare up, and they couldn't wait to get back to school to tell us of their success, and *quod erat demonstrandum*.

The Skillit boys were quite likeable personalities, but although it was easy to see that they were brothers, they were different in many respects. Skull, unlike Tim, had a lithe physique, and was a good athlete. He had a lot of success in the annual school sports, and did a good job representing the school for a while as centre forward in the football team.

There was a boy called Al Mean in the school with whom NOBODY would argue, not even Skull.

Al had a head shaped like an upside down plant pot, a barrel chest, and very wide, broad shoulders —— he was in fact built like a tank. He would have made a good "minder" or "enforcer" for a top Mafia Godfather.

However, as no one questioned Al's authority, he led quite a peaceful life, and deep down he was a good man at heart.

In his own quiet way, he did what he could to protect the school's image when there was activity which could have had an adverse impact on its reputation.

Quite a long time after I had left the school, I visited the Old Boys' Club, and Al was there as an enthusiastic volunteer promoting the interests of the club. He was pleased to see me again and made me feel very much at home with his warm and friendly welcome.

A number of boys, who were in the form above us, were held back, i.e. relegated to our class because of poor results, and so we had the benefit of their company.

Two of these students were Jackie Northerland and Thomas Hebron. One day Jackie noticed Thomas was scratching his bum during a lesson, and passed him a note telling him he was a dirty bugger. This note was intercepted by Mr. McKenna (Black Bart), the history teacher, who proceeded to read it out as an example of dreadful behaviour.

Black Bart was on a perpetual mission to improve the boys' standard of manners and moral behaviour. For example when he heard a sound indicating one of the students had a wind problem, he lectured at great length about etiquette, and recommended more pepper on food as an aid to control flatulence.

Black Bart was also known as Mucky McKenna, in view of his habitual ardent nose picking, and scratching of his arse, whilst energetically, but unsuccessfully, trying to impart his own dubious brand of knowledge into the minds of sceptical students.

John Flynn (Flynnie) was another boy demoted to our form. Flynnie was a good natural story teller, and mimic, with a lively sense of humour. His Father ran the Castle and Anchor pub in Stockton, just across the road from the Globe Theatre; a big venue for stand up comedians, who performed to audiences in excess of 2,000 people. After the show these entertainers called at Flynnie's pub for late night drinks, and proceeded to tell the jokes which were not suitable for consumption by the general public. Flynnie entertained us by passing these stories on to us at school.

Flynnie was a good footballer, and a regular in the school team. He moved with the ball close to his feet, with a characteristic shuffle, which cleverly disguised his lack of pace.

Billy Baldwin (Baldy) was another boy with a good sense of humour, which was just as well, because he tended to get himself into difficulties. One day Big Bill asked,

"Baldwin, *snort*, *snort*, go to the lab, *snort*, *snort*, and bring me some paper".

Baldy must have misheard this request because instead of going to the laboratory, he went to the lavatory and brought back a toilet roll.

Mr. Barnwell (Barney) was the chemistry teacher in charge of the lab. He had purposely developed a strict, disciplinarian reputation, and had a severe expression on his face, as he peered through his very thick horn rimmed glasses. This enabled him to have complete control in classes; but occasionally he displayed another side to his character, when his face would break into a warm smile. He was a good teacher, and gave good advice before exams,

"If you sacrifice your leisure time, and apply yourselves to study now, you will get good results, and this sense of achievement will be a source of a special kind of happiness".

Barney was good to me in another way,

because he believed I was a useful footballer and, when I was in form four, arranged for me to play for the seniors.

Barney's opinions were respected by Father Cunningham (Foxy), and when these two agreed on a subject they had a strong influence.

Foxy was a sports' enthusiast, and made sure the school's teams turned out in style, with first class kit. In the big annual athletics' gala, when the local schools in the County competed against each other, we didn't win much because the other schools were a lot bigger, but we always looked the most professional in our immaculate pale blue track suits.

A notable annual event was the cricket match, when a team from the sixth form and teachers, played a select eleven from the rest of the school.

Foxy was a distinguished sportsman with a Cambridge "blue" for rowing; and also a quality cricketer.

One year he came out to bat with his Cambridge cap and spotless whites, and made his way down the veranda steps at the back of the school, along the path through the rear garden lawns, and all the way out to the wicket where he took up his stance to receive the first ball. In a most professional manner he padded the ball away, only to be given out, LBW, with an extremely dubious decision from one of the senior boys acting as umpire. He grimaced, ground his teeth together, and proceeded to make the long walk back across the field, through the garden lawns, and then up the veranda steps, and to his own room in the school.

Cricket can be a very cruel game.

My brother Trevor was a good athlete, and he won the trophy for the best overall performance at the school's annual sports' day. He also played a great game at centre half, at Darlington AFC's ground, in an inter-school cup final. It was a soaking wet day but Dad, Mam, and I were there as part of a good crowd to watch the match.

The school's football house encounters were big events. There was a good atmosphere at these matches as the whole school turned out to watch the games.

For a couple of years we had a particularly good senior team. We won almost every game, and had the satisfaction of beating St. Cuthbert's from Newcastle on both occasions, when we played them at home and away. This was a good achievement because they had a lot of pupils in their school, and were noted for the strength of their football teams.

Trevor loved the school and never wanted to leave, and stayed for three years after "O" levels, most of which he spent sun bathing on the grassy bank behind the main football pitch during the long, hot, sunny summers.

Trevor always enjoyed good weather, and one of his particular interests in life is meteorology. His favourite TV programme is the weather forecast; he never misses it.

Mr. Anderson (Gandhi), the art teacher, was a gifted artist, but not too bright in other respects. He was called Gandhi because his facial features were an exact double for the distinguished Indian leader.

He had very little control over the boys in the classroom, but somehow managed to get good exam results by demonstrating to us various artistic tricks and skills.

We sat there struggling with a pictorial composition of very poor quality, when he appeared over our shoulder with,

"Coom 'ere lad",

and taking the paint brush from our hand, deftly inserted on the picture some feature, like a rural fence between fields, which immediately transformed the whole thing into a work of art, in just a few seconds.

Mr. Pybus (Danny), the English teacher, also had very little classroom control, but used his enthusiasm for his subject to inspire us. In reading "Great Expectations" his clever interpretations gave us a marvellous insight into Dickens' exceptional descriptive powers.

However, I got into trouble in one of Danny's classes, and was suspended from the school just before the final examinations.

Mam was required to come to the school with me for an audience with Foxy.

This was a tense occasion,

"Well Mrs Heslop, you know why you have been called to see me?"

"Yes, Harry has told us he was suspended for smoking and playing cards at the back of the English class".

"No, Mrs. Heslop, that is not why Harry was suspended".

"No?"

"No, he was suspended for disobedience".

"Disobedience?"

"Yes, disobedience. He had already been told previously, not to smoke and play cards during lessons".

I had been a silly little fool and could have been expelled, and been unable to sit the GCE exams. This would effectively mean having wasted all my time at the school.

Fortunately for me Foxy proved to be a warm hearted and wise man---he knew he couldn't appear to condone my actions which clearly had shown disrespect to the good teacher, so he focussed on my disobedience as the main fault, and was thus able to imply that the suspension, rather than expulsion, from school was sufficient punishment.

He was very good to me; I was reinstated, and did OK in the final exams, before leaving school for the last time.

I had no idea what kind of job I should go for, or what I was going to do with the rest of my life.

However, more by accident than design, I went on to have the kind of eventful and unusual life which I could never have anticipated at that time.

END OF PART ONE.

Arry Eslop, Part Two

Diary of the
Early Adult Years

*For my brother Trevor who loved the school,
and invariably won the slow bicycle races by
skilfully finishing last.*

7

THE ARICLED CLERK, 1956 TO 1961

The first part of this book was written in the first person, because the author felt comfortable writing subjectively about when he was a child, but the second part, when he was an adult, sounds more natural in the objective, third person. The author has therefore used the third person for the rest of the story.

Also in future Arry Eslop will be referred to as Harry.

After leaving school Harry had very little idea what he was going to do for a living. His Father seemed to like the idea of him joining his insurance broking firm, so he arranged for Harry to go off to work in the Newcastle branch of a large insurance company to learn the business. He was bored stiff, and after a few days went to see the branch manager to say he was sorry, but this work was clearly not for him.

Harry then learned that his lifelong friend, Michael Jeffery, who was the same age as him (he was four days older and had come through all the same school classes with Harry) had become an articled clerk with a local firm of Chartered Accountants, and appeared to be happy there.

Harry applied to join this firm as an articled clerk, and it was agreed that he had the appropriate qualifications to be accepted and to study to become a Chartered Accountant by correspondence course. The articles were for a period of five years with the object of sitting the final accountancy exam at the end of that term.

The starting salary was £1 10s 0d per week rising to five pounds per week in the fifth year. This was quite a good deal at the time, because just prior to that year it was required to pay a premium to become articled, and the articled clerk received no salary at all.

This change to an accountancy career proved to be a big step in the right direction for Harry because it was a happy firm, and the articled clerks shared their own big room in an old Victorian office building.

There were time sheets to fill in each week, but there was a fairly ad hoc approach to this discipline, and always plenty of time to admire the pretty girls walking by in the street below the office. Nevertheless, Harry received a first class training in the nuts and bolts of accountancy at the coal face.

Local trade's people would come into the office with a big cardboard box full of scruffy invoices, bank statements, cheque book counterfoils, etc. And then, as if by magic, this mixed up jumble of papers would be turned into a beautiful set of accounts, profit & loss a/c and balance sheet. This was all very much appreciated by the Inland Revenue when the accounts were submitted for the client's tax return, even though the Inspector of Taxes realised that the numbers had been well and truly massaged in such a way as to reduce the client's tax liability to the absolute minimum.

There were some older, experienced employees in the office who were not qualified, but had a natural gift for accountancy; they were able to give the articled clerks the value of their wealth of experience. It was a great place to learn the beauty of the logic of double entry book-keeping. This proved to be the right career path for Harry because he soon began to realise that he had a natural ability in this field.

He was reminded that when in form one at school, the maths teacher gave him a mark of 99 out of 100, and said the mark should really have been 100%, but he only gave him 99% because NOBODY ever gets 100%.

These were happy, relaxed years in the office, but the accountancy course was taken very seriously, and involved many hours of concentrated study at home.

The old Victorian office was a most peculiar and strange building. In fact, if a camel could be described as a horse created by a committee, then it would have been quite natural to assume that this office building had been designed by a similar process. There were many strange aspects to the structure; halfway down the stairs from the top floor, there was a very long and wide flight of stairs that ran off at a right angle to the main staircase. It then appeared to go nowhere. But at the bottom of the stairs, there was a single door which gave access to a single cubicle Victorian-style lavatory. This was indeed a peculiar place to build a toilet.

When one gentleman in particular used the facility, an awful smell would drift up and waft around the whole building.

It was said that the office had originally been built as an hotel many years ago, and was used by businessmen on overnight stays in the town. In those days, heavy industry, particularly coal mining, was thriving in the area. The owners of the mines were wealthy people, who could use a good central hotel for their meetings. Their wealth would account for the extravagant use of space in the building; the rooms were enormous, particularly the one later used by the articled clerks. This would have been a very large and expensive bedroom when the building was an hotel.

But in other respects the hotel must have looked a bit like a Wild West saloon. It brought to mind images of outlaws falling through the stairs' banister onto the wide landing below, after being shot by the town sheriff.

The senior partners in the firm were quite old, and had some very sound economical ways, no doubt influenced by the food shortages experienced during the Second World War.

When making the morning tea, one of the partners would insist that the teapot should be taken to the kettle, and NOT the kettle to the teapot. This ensured that the water was boiling hot when it was poured onto the tea, and the maximum flavour was extracted from the minimum tea.

Harry and the other articled clerks had a carefree time in the office, and fooled around to keep themselves entertained. This did not help to promote the professional image of the firm, particularly when they answered the phone with made up locations; a favourite was "Chessington Zoo". These frivolous games caused the clients to believe they had called the wrong number. They were not amused, but for some reason the clerks never received any adverse feedback from the partners in the firm.

These were relaxed, happy-go-lucky times.

Harry liked to have a thorough understanding of a subject from the ground up. He had the same approach to accountancy, and asked a lot of questions in the office.

One thing that puzzled him was the description of a bank statement balance, because assets such as cash at bank were debit balances in the client's balance sheet, whereas the client's bank statement would show this cash at bank as a credit balance. He didn't always receive a quick answer to this kind of question. In this particular instance the client's bank statement is expressing the balance from the bank's point of view, i.e. it is a credit balance on the bank statement because the client is a creditor of the bank.

In 1960
Michael Jeffery (on the right) with Harry in the office
pretending to be "B movie" gangsters.

8

THE HOLIDAYS, 1956 TO 1959

It was a friendly office, with the staff sharing social evenings and going on holidays together.

On one occasion eight of them hired a boat on the Norfolk Broads.

This was an interesting experience when they navigated the boat to Norwich and Great Yarmouth, calling at rural pubs on the way.

They had great difficulty mooring the craft in the Great Yarmouth harbour, where there was a strong current from the outgoing tide. The vessel was soon completely out of control, and spinning around in a most chaotic and alarming fashion.

Various people, who looked like proper sailors, were shouting instructions from the quayside to try to help them, no doubt worried about the risk of collateral damage to the other boats in the harbour. After some time a rope was got on board, and the craft was then able to be safely moored by the quayside.

At the end of this holiday Harry had a bad time.

He caught Asian flu on the journey home, and was unconscious for three days. He woke up to see his Mother and the family doctor peering down at him through the steam rising from his body. They were relieved to see him awake again.

This was a particularly dangerous strain of flu which claimed a lot of lives in the UK that year.

After this, Harry gradually regained his strength, and returned to the office where life went on in the same old carefree way.

However, early in the 1956 summer, he received a phone call from his old school friends who had stayed on to study in form six.

Although there was no official school camping holiday that year, they had obtained permission to use the school's camping equipment, and were going to the regular camp site near Richmond in Yorkshire. It was in a farmer's field on a bank that ran down to the beautiful River Swale.

Harry jumped at this opportunity to join his friends because he had always loved the school camp.

When he was in form one, his fellow campers thought he made a very good cup of tea, and he had become the official tea maker. This freed him from the less pleasant chores, like peeling the potatoes.

The camp equipment included a very large kettle and a very large tea pot, so there was some skill required in ensuring that the water heated on the camp fire was boiling hot, and gauging how much tea to use in the teapot.

It was a pleasant walk into Richmond, which was only about two miles from the campsite. While there, they visited a cafe in the market place, and played the new Elvis songs on the jukebox. This was the first time they heard him singing, "Teddy Bear", "Heartbreak Hotel", and "All Shook Up".

It was the start of rock and roll.

The following year Harry received a call from his friends who had gone on to study at Newcastle University. They were planning a hitch-hiking holiday in Germany, visiting beer festivals on the way, and Harry joined them.

The country had already made good progress in recovering from the impact of the war, and the people were friendly and tolerant towards Harry and his friends. They referred to themselves as "The Danker Boys", because "danke" was the only word they knew in the German language.

The beer at the festival was strong and served in litre-size steins.

Very soon the boys were quite drunk, so they decided to move on to the next village by train.

However, this proved to be a non-stop express to communist East Germany. Fortunately, when their tickets were checked they were still in West Germany, and the ticket inspector allowed them off the train just before it passed through the Iron Curtain into the East.

To get a break from accountancy studies, Harry sometimes went to visit his friends who were now students at Newcastle University.

Usually they watched Newcastle United play at St. James' Park on the Saturday afternoon, before having a few bottles of Newcastle

Brown Ale in the Bun Room at the Students' Union. They would then head off to a party, normally in Jesmond, where most of the students had their accommodation.

There was always an open invitation for the nurses at the RVI Hospital, as this provided a good boy/girl balance at the parties.

9

FOOTBALL, 1955 TO 1957

When Harry left school he was lucky to be living in the right place at the right time. Living in Bishop Auckland he could watch the "Bishops" in their heyday - they played first-class football in front of big crowds.

There was a total gate of close to 200,000 for the 1954 Amateur Cup Final between Bishop Auckland and Crook Town. A crowd of 100,000 watched the first game at Wembley, with the match finishing 2-2 after extra time.

Crook Town is only about five miles from Bishop Auckland, so British Rail had a major logistics problem in transporting all the fans from these two towns to London. Nevertheless, they did a brilliant job.

Two or three weeks before the Wembley final, British Rail began marshalling long trains of coaches in the railway sidings at the two stations. Then all through the Friday night before the match, these steam trains - which carried over 20,000 supporters - headed south to London. British Rail even provided full English breakfasts on the journey.

The first replay was at St. James' Park, Newcastle, where over 56,000 fans saw the game again drawn 2-2 after extra time.

The second replay was at Ayresome Park, Middlesbrough, with a gate of 37,000. Crook Town won this second replay 1-0.

This ONE cup tie attracted a total crowd of nearly 200,000.

Harry was at all three games.

In 1955, 1956, and 1957 the "Bishops" had a hat-trick of amateur cup wins at Wembley. The outside rights in these three finals all went on to play for Football League clubs; Major went to Hull City, McKenna to Leeds United, and Bradley to Manchester United.

Many other "Bishops" players became famous in the top Football League. Laurie Brown, for example, became a popular regular with Arsenal, playing for them both at centre half and centre forward.

A particularly remarkable player was inside forward Seamus O'Connell. He played sufficient games for Chelsea to win a Champion's medal in 1955, when Chelsea won the top flight for the first time. He did this at the same time that he was winning Amateur Cup winners medals (in 1955 and 1956) while playing for the "Bishops".

He should have been known as football's

"Have gun ... will travel".

However, the most notable of the team's players was Bobby Hardisty. He will always be remembered as Mr. Bishop Auckland. For many years he was the backbone of the team, as well as being the most highly rated England Amateur International of all time. It was rumoured that Bobby never accepted a penny to reimburse his expenses in case it jeopardised his amateur status.

It was about then that Harry was signed on by the "Bishops", but he only played a handful of games at the end of each of the seasons he was there, when the team was trying to clear the backlog of fixtures that had accumulated after its successful runs in all competitions. Nevertheless, he enjoyed training with the team at their Kingsway ground on Tuesday and Thursday nights.

10

THE STREET PAPER SELLER, 1955

Harry applied to sell "The Football Pink" on the streets of Bishop Auckland on Saturday nights. The Pink was published in Darlington, and it competed with Middlesbrough's Sports Gazette. He was accepted as a "Football Pink" street seller, and started work the following Saturday.

This was thought to be a very low grade, menial job.

At first Harry felt embarrassed as he walked down the main street selling his papers, but he felt better when he reminded himself he would usually earn around £2.00 for about four hours work. This contrasted with the boys who delivered the papers every day, who had to get out of bed at six o'clock in the morning and were paid only £0.10s.0d (ten shillings, or fifty pence in today's money) for the full week's work.

One Boxing Day the Sports Gazette was not published, but Harry was out selling the Pink. The "Bishops" were playing at home at Kingsway, and he sold in the ground with the half-time scores, and then on the street as usual in the evening.

When he cashed in that night he was told he had earned a record amount of £3.17s.6d. This was a remarkable sum for about five hours work.

The papers were two old pence each, and the seller received 25% commission, i.e. one half pence per paper sold. As there were 480 half pence to the Pound Sterling, this represented a sale of 1,860 newspapers.

As a street seller doesn't need a shop, he has no overhead expenses.

This income of £3.17s.6d. in one evening was also a lot more than the £1.10s.0d. per week Harry was earning as an articled clerk.

It follows that Harry never found himself short of beer money. A pint of Newcastle

Breweries' IPA cost one Shilling (Five Pence in today's money), and it could be enjoyed in very comfortable surroundings - sitting in leather armchairs in the lounge bar of the Crows' Nest pub in the Haymarket, in the centre of Newcastle-upon-Tyne.

One particularly memorable evening when Harry was selling his sports papers on Newgate Street outside of Rossi's milk bar, a message came through that the "Bishops" first team were short of one player for their evening game at Kingsway - Harry was asked if he would go and play.

He immediately left his newspapers in the care of the milk bar, and ran around to the ground. Twenty minutes later Harry was turning out with the first team, and playing in his favourite outside right position.

There was a good crowd in the ground for an end of season game. Bishops won, and Harry thought he played well. At the end of the match, Michael Jeffery's brother, David, ran onto the pitch and asked him for his autograph. Harry thought he couldn't be serious, but as David handed him a pen, he signed his autograph.

After the bath, Harry changed, and was about to set off home when Corbet Cresswell (a first-class centre-half sought after by teams in the top flight of the English Football League) asked where he was going. Harry told him he was going home. Corbet said,

"No don't do that yet, you should join this queue outside of the Treasurer's office and stand behind me".

When it came to Harry's turn, the Treasurer said he would need his expenses, and handed him £7.0s.0d. Harry was more than happy with this, and went home feeling ten feet tall and walking on air.

He quickly went up the steep hill to the house because he wanted to tell his parents about the events of the evening ... they usually came to watch when he was playing.

He found his Dad and Mam, and Bisto the cat, in the lounge in front of a roaring fire, watching Dixon of Dock Green on a small black and white TV. When he told them what had happened, they were amazed, but also very pleased and proud.

This year was the highlight of Harry's very short football career. At the age of seventeen, he hadn't reached a sufficient level of physical fitness to play a high standard of football on a regular basis.

He was also aware that his first priority was to concentrate on his studies, to try to qualify as a Chartered Accountant so he could start earning a proper living.

11

THE FRIEND, 1945 TO 1989

When Harry was five years old he started school at St. Wilfred's in Bishop Auckland, and it was there that he met Michael Jeffery (Jeff) for the first time. In a remarkable sequence of events, this was to become a strong and lasting friendship.

Jeff was a very clever boy, and even at that young age, when they had just started school, he gave Harry some sound advice:

"When answering a question, don't keep going on at great length; just keep the answer short and to the point."

In other words what he was saying was:

"Quit while you are ahead."

This was a clever observation for a five-year-old boy.

When they were about nine years old, Jeff's

uncle, who lived in Jersey, invited the boys to spend a holiday with him. This was agreed, and Harry and Jeff soon found themselves in the uncle's car, on the way to stay at his place. It was a great adventure for the young boys.

Jersey was a lovely island. It had made a quick recovery from the trauma of Germany's occupation during the Second World War.

They all explored the island and visited the underground hospital built by prisoners during the war. It was no longer used as a hospital, but had become more of a tourist attraction.

Jeff's uncle liked fishing, and showed the boys some of the finer arts of the sport.

Harry didn't really want to catch fish, as he didn't like the idea of killing them. However, he couldn't stop catching them, and kept calling for help to land them off his line ... meanwhile, Jeff and his uncle caught nothing.

The day before returning to England, Jeff's uncle said to him,

"If you can avoid smoking until you are twenty one years old, I will give you £100".

At that time smoking was fashionable. Film stars were rarely seen without a cigarette in their hand, thus providing a big free advertisement for the cigarette industry.

In those days it was not unusual to start smoking before leaving school, and Jeff was smoking Capstain Full Strength well before he reached the age of twenty one. Needless to say, he never collected the £100 from his uncle.

Harry and Jeff went through junior school together, and then passed the scholarship for the grammar school, where they both played for the same school football and cricket teams.

In school exams Jeff always got the better marks. Harry thought he had a photographic memory, as he seemed to achieve everything without any effort.

After leaving school, they were both articled to the same firm of Chartered Accountants, and then sat the final accountancy exams at the same time, in November 1961.

Earlier that year they had jointly celebrated their twenty first birthdays, with a big party at the Heslop household in Bishop Auckland. Harry's parents were away on holiday in Devon at the time.

In later years, everything went wrong for Jeff.

He was living and working in New Zealand, with his wife and young family, when his wife became ill with a rare form of skin disease. Tragically, she then died.

Jeff was devastated, and brought his family back to the UK, where he landed a job as Chief Accountant for a large company based in Manchester.

He married again and was happy for a while, but was later diagnosed with cancer, and died shortly before his fiftieth birthday.

At that time Harry was celebrating his fiftieth birthday with a party at his home in Surrey. His brother Trevor was there; though he had heard the news that Jeff had just died, Trevor didn't tell anyone until later, as he didn't want the party to become a sad occasion.

The news shocked Harry ... there were so many cruel and sad times in Jeff's short life.

Jeff's early death was a tragedy. He was a great character, highly thought of, quiet and thoughtful. He adopted a low profile, but his intelligence and humour enriched the lives of everyone he met.

12

THE GIRLFRIEND, 1956/57

There was only one telephone in the big room used by the articled clerks. It could, therefore, be embarrassing making a call to a girl to fix a date, as everyone in the room listened in on the conversation.

Three of the clerks had had a public school education, and though this had given them more self confidence than the other employees, even they were still nervous on the phone when ringing a girl for the first time.

Harry and the other staff, who didn't have the benefit of the self confidence taught in public schools, found these calls to girls quite nerve racking.

This was most apparent when Harry rang a girl he had first seen from the office widow.

He thought she was lovely; a most attractive and elegant girl, with perfect poise and posture. She could have been an inspiration for Roy Orbison's song "Pretty Woman".

She had blonde hair with a fringe, and reminded Harry of Zoe Newton, who was a model commissioned to portray good health for the British Milk Marketing Board.

Harry plucked up courage and made the call; he was delighted when she agreed to go to the cinema with him.

He didn't have a car so couldn't take a girl for a drive in the countryside. Fortunately she liked going to the pictures, but Harry thought that wasn't as sociable as visiting a pub, where there is more chance to talk and get to know each other.

The next time they had a date, he met her off the bus as usual, and as they strolled towards the cinema, Anne (that was the girl's name) mentioned that she did ballet from the age of eight until she was fifteen. Harry told her he thought she had perfect posture, and the ballet must have helped in this respect.

When he told her this she seemed pleased.

They went to the pictures quite a lot.

One day Harry took her to see his old school, and this involved a long walk from the bus. They became quite tired that afternoon so, to avoid more walking, that evening they went to see James Dean in the film "Giant".

The next day in the office, Harry received a humorous Valentine's card from Anne. It was a bit rude but very funny. He thought it was the best Valentine's card he had ever received. In fact, it may well have been the ONLY Valentine's card he had ever received.

This particular card was quite a topic of conversation in the office.

There is no doubt he loved Anne a lot, but thought she wouldn't want to hear that, so he didn't tell her.

One outing to the cinema was a fiasco. Anne went skipping up the stairs to find seats, while Harry paid for the tickets. They were three shillings each. All he had in his pocket was three two-shilling pieces - the exact total cost. Sadly, the cashier said one of these coins was South African, and couldn't accept it in payment.

He chased after Anne and explained the situation. They then went all the way up to his parents' house for some more money, before going on to a different cinema; Harry was too embarrassed to go back to the Odeon.

This whole business didn't seem to bother

Anne.

They continued going out together, but sadly after a while they drifted apart, and went their own separate ways.

He knew he wasn't in a position to look after her, because it would be almost five years before he could qualify, and start earning a proper living.

She had been Harry's first girlfriend.

1956/57

Harry's first girlfriend —— Anne

13

THE FINAL EXAMS, 1961

There were two sets of exams for students studying to become members of the Institute of Chartered Accountants.

After about 2½ years there was the "Intermediate", which involved six 3-hour papers taken in three days; two papers each day, one in the morning and one in the afternoon.

Then, after another 2½ years, at the end of the term of articles, there were the "Finals". These were seven 3-hour papers to be completed in 3½ days.

These exams were recognised to be very tough, and stressful. If you passed them you were a big success, but if you failed just one of the papers you were a complete failure, and had to start all over again.

There was a lot of pressure. They had to work quickly to complete the papers in the allotted time, and pass marks were required in all papers. If one was failed then all seven had to be taken again.

Harry religiously kept to the study timetable, and some weeks before the finals gave himself mock exams, in examination conditions, using actual previous exam papers. He also attended a residential course on some aspects of accountancy at Durham University.

He kept himself as fit as possible. About six months before the exams, he gave up smoking --- he had read somewhere that it could dull the brain.

The exam venue for students from the North East of England was in a hall at a junction of five roads, just on the entry to Gateshead after leaving Low Fell.

There was a church at the end of each of these five roads, so the locals called the junction "Amen Corner".

These exams were in November 1961.

The weather in the North East at that time of the year can be severe, so to avoid the possibility of travel disruptions, Harry arranged to stay at his Auntie Norah's place in

Low Fell throughout the period of the exams. Her house was within walking distance of the centre to be used for the exams.

In fact, at the time of the exams the weather was cold, but dry and bright, so Harry had a refreshing walk to the centre each day.

He knew he had done everything possible to enable him to perform to the best of his ability, but after completing the exam papers he didn't know whether or not he had been successful...he would just have to wait for the results to come out.

Harry and Jeff returned to the office, and immediately surprised everyone by announcing they were leaving to go to live and work in London.

They both used an agency to find accountancy jobs in the City.

Jeff found accommodation in the Hampstead area, and Harry went to live in Notting Hill.

They were to be living in London when the results of their final accountancy exams came out.

END OF PART TWO

Arry Eslop – Part Three

Living in London

For My Wife, Anne

With Lots of Love

Harry with his wife Anne, son Mark and baby daughter Rachael, in the garden of their home in Bermuda in 1972.

Part one, two, three and four of the Arry Eslop story in this book cover his life only up to the year 1964, before he returned to the North East of England, after living in Africa.

He married Anne in Bishop Auckland in 1968, and after a short honeymoon in the Lake District, went to live and work in Bermuda in September 1968.

The years after 1964 in the Arry Eslop story will be covered in a later edition.

14

LEAVING FOR LONDON

Harry's Dad went with him to see him off at Bishop Auckland station to catch the little steam train to Darlington, where he was to change for the main line train to London, King's Cross.

This was in January 1962 when British Railways' trains were still hauled by steam locomotives, whereas countries like Germany and France had taken the bold and more practical move to the use of diesel and electric trains.

The UK government had made the decision to stick with steam because of the shortage of capital to convert to more efficient engines, following the crippling cost of the 1939/45 Second World War.

The UK was therefore still a paradise for

steam enthusiasts, and with the country having plenty of relatively cheap coal it seemed like an appropriate way to proceed at that time.

Harry loved the sense of adventure experienced when travelling by steam trains. He enjoyed the journey to King's Cross where there was always a sense of excitement and a buzz of expectation in the big city, which contrasted to the quiet and more rural life he had left behind in Bishop Auckland.

Mainline railway stations always seemed livelier in those days, with porters and passengers rushing around, and the impatient panting of the engines with a mixture of steam and smoke, and then appearing to give a sigh of relief after completing their long journeys.

Harry had been asked if he would be interested in sharing a flat with Frank a boy he had known at school who was now living with three other colleagues, all of whom had known each other when they were students at Birmingham University.

The flat was north of Notting Hill Gate, so Harry went straight to the Underground to catch a Hammersmith and City line train to Ladbroke Grove station.

He noticed the rural sounding names of the Tube stations on this line, such as Royal Oak, Westbourne Park, Shepherd's Bush, and Goldhawk Road, which seemed to belong to times gone by, before the sprawl into the countryside from London's nonstop expansion.

This part of West London had for some years been completely absorbed into the Metropolis, and it was now a quite run down bed-sitter area, compared to its salubrious status in the Victorian era.

Harry got off the train at Ladbroke Grove station, and soon found the flat nearby in Bassett Road, where he was given a warm welcome and a cup of tea, before they all went out for a couple of beers at one of their local pubs, The Kensington Park Hotel (known simply as the KPH).

It was difficult to visualise this establishment as an hotel because it was no more than a small "gin palace" pub, with a variety of customers, some of questionable character.

Nevertheless, at that time it was well run by an Irish landlord who took pride in serving a good pint of beer. In the early 1960s there were a lot of Irish publicans doing a good job in London pubs.

It was a good era for pop records; the pub's juke box was always playing, and there was a warm and friendly atmosphere.

It was usually quite busy, particularly when the commuters were returning home after work in the City. But the regulars were in the pub whenever it was open. There was Taffy, the Welsh prostitute who was a very good looking, buxom young woman, and also an Irishman called Hammer who appeared to be a part-time pimp for Taffy, as he didn't seem to have any other job. However he did have a surprisingly lucrative and rather unusual form of alternative income.

In those days to make a call from a public call box, the caller inserted four pence into the phone box; then if he had a connection he pressed button (A) in order to hear the person to whom he wished to speak. However if there was no reply he would press button (B) to retrieve his four pence from the phone. Hammer used this system to his advantage.

When the weather was pleasant he strolled around the streets of the area and placed wedges in the button (B) outlet to prevent the coins being returned when the call was not connected. About one week later, again assuming it was a pleasant day for a stroll; he would go round to the same call boxes and remove the wedges to allow the accumulated pennies to fall out; a bit like hitting the jackpot on a fruit machine. It was not unusual to see him pay for all his drinks in pence.

Hammer and Taffy were always in the pub sitting at the bar near the juke box; they appeared to be quite content to live for today as though there was no tomorrow, and had no interest in straying from their home patch near the KPH.

If Taffy liked a particular record she would keep herself entertained by having a little dance to the music with the other customers.

She would, however, walk up to Ladbroke Grove station to meet her clients when they were returning home on the commuter trains.

These "clients" were quite anonymous because in the early 1960s office workers in London, from managing directors to filing clerks, all looked alike with their black bowler hats and rolled umbrellas. This way of dressing was like a uniform, but it caused confusion, and numerous hats and brollies finished up in the lost property offices.

Notting Hill Gate has now become a place where wealthy people will pay huge prices for their apartments, because it has acquired a reputation as THE place to live for high-flying City dealers and brokers, but it has lost a lot of the character and charm which it had when it was NOT the place to live in the early 1960s, which was the time when Harry lived there.

This was not long after the Notting Hill race riots which had received wide publicity and given the area a bad image.

However London has a remarkable capacity for reinventing itself, and a calmer atmosphere had developed in the area.

There was still a friendly atmosphere around Portobello Road where many of the local people, and shop keepers, had lived for generations. Sadly these days there is a clear dividing line between the "posh" area of Notting Hill, and the "not posh" part, and Ladbroke Grove and the KPH would fall into the latter category. However, it is this latter category that gives a feel for how the area was in the early 1960s when there was a seductive atmosphere throughout the whole of Notting Hill.

As Harry and his new flat mates walked back from the pub, he felt comfortable in his new surroundings, and the flat he was to share with the other boys was quite pleasant. He looked forward to a new experience living in London.

When he had settled in he particularly enjoyed shopping in the family run grocery shops at the north end of Portobello Road, where he bought good quality ham for his breakfasts.

Also he kept his laundry as simple as possible. At that time people working in the City wore collar detached shirts, so he bought seven collars for each shirt. When he went to the launderette in Westbourne Grove his washing didn't take long, but he still had time to pop into the pub next door for a drink, before going back to pick up his laundry.

15

WORK IN LONDON

The following day Harry had arranged to have an interview with a City firm of chartered accountants with offices near Moorgate station. This was convenient because the Underground would take him all the way from Ladbroke Grove without changing trains.

The interview with the senior partner went well, and he was offered a job starting the following Monday.

There was always a demand for part-qualified accountants who were waiting for the results of their final examinations.

This was a busy time of the year for the firm because they were involved in the year end audits.

On Harry's first day he was part of a team auditing the accounts of a big international bank. The audit was shared with an international firm of accountants, because the firm Harry was with was not big enough to cover the wide scope of the client's business.

Harry and the other audit staff were accommodated in a large and luxurious boardroom in the client's head office in the City.

The partner managing the audit for the firm which had employed Harry explained the programme and how they were to proceed with the work. His name was Edgerton and the manager of the other joint auditor was called Frobisher.

They both had the appearance of men who had been born for careers in the City. Edgerton, in particular, was the ultimate City gent with his pin-striped suit, bowler hat, rolled umbrella, and a complexion with a shiny and healthy glow, acquired from the exercise in walking across London Bridge to the office every day.

Edgerton and Frobisher appeared to be on the same wave length as they strutted around the boardroom discussing the finer points of the audit.

They were concerned with a high level of fine tuning, and went to great lengths to decide whether one part of the annual report should include the word "and" or "or". Harry thought it was silly to make a fuss about such little details.

As the day progressed it transpired that this part of the audit involved reviewing reports from the client's Far East managers, to "take a view" on the level of bad debts provision that should be in the accounts.

(This expression "take a view" has become even more prevalent over the years, and can produce results which are wildly inaccurate, and could cause accountants to lose credibility. However, this should not be confused with the connotation "taking a broad brush approach" which is a term often used by accountants when producing a quick result, which is usually very accurate and remarkably close to the final official audited result.)

The Far East managers described some extremely dubious debtors, such as undischarged bankrupt alcoholics, saying they were sure the customer would repay the loan, and recommended that no bad debt provision was required.

As the auditors were sitting in London, thousands of miles away, they were not in a position to debate the point, so they simply wrote off 100% of the debt.

Under these circumstances it seemed there was little chance of preparing an accurate set of accounts, and Harry thought this rendered Edgerton and Frobisher's discussions on fine tuning the balance sheet quite ridiculous.

Edgerton was like a caricature of the archetypal City of London accountant, but he appeared to have led quite a sheltered life, only commuting to and from London, and totally focused on his work.

However, he maintained a pleasant working environment with his friendly personality.

When Harry had completed his first week on this audit, Edgerton called everyone to a meeting to tell them that they were going to carry out a surprise cash count at one of the bank's larger UK branches.

It transpired that the branch was in Whitehall near Westminster Bridge. He explained that they were all to meet as inconspicuously as possible, in a side street near the bank.

Everyone had to be there at precisely 9.30 am to hear how he planned to conduct the operation.

The next day Harry made sure he was on time, and Edgerton explained that when he gave the order to "GO", they were all to get into the bank immediately, get behind the counter, and tell the bank staff to stand clear, because this was a surprise audit cash count.

When Edgerton and the team moved in it was like an SAS raid...the bank's staff were terrified, and the whole operation developed into a spectacular farce.

Eventually Harry found himself in the bank's vaults, asking for large packages of newly minted notes to be opened so that he could count them.

At the end of the exercise Edgerton seemed satisfied he had achieved the objective; presumably he was aware of the cash value that was to be expected.

Harry enjoyed this visit to the West End for the surprise cash count which was an unusual and unique experience. It was refreshing to have a break from the mind numbing work in the bank's head office in the City, where he thought they were involved in a completely useless exercise.

He had become disheartened with this work, and felt he needed to get involved in something practical in order to preserve his sanity.

To achieve this he took an evening job as a barman in a pub near Westminster Cathedral in Victoria. He began to feel quite useful again when he was serving pints of beer in the public bar.

He wasn't so comfortable working in the lounge bar where the rounds of drinks tended to be much more complicated.

There was a hospital nearby and a lot of the lounge bar customers were doctors from that establishment and they were usually accompanied by nurses who ordered fancy drinks which were confusing for the barmen.

One of the benefits of this job was a meal from the kitchen. It was just something simple, like sausage, beans and chips, but it ensured the barmen had something in their stomachs.

It was a long working day, with two jobs; one in the City and one in the pub at night, and Harry felt very tired by the time he climbed into bed.

Leaving the pub at the "death" just before midnight, he caught one of the late number 52 buses from Victoria to Notting Hill Gate and Ladbroke Grove.

He was then up early the next day to get back to the bank to continue working on the audit.

The barman job had helped to bring Harry back to the real world, and to preserve his sanity, but after a couple of weeks he thought he was trying to do too much, and decided to give up the job at the pub.

After that he relaxed at night with a few pints in the KPH, where Hammer offered him cannabis, and assured him it was of the highest quality.

Taffy was also very friendly, and said Harry was quite welcome to sleep with her free of charge.

He thanked them both for their offers, but declined their invitations.

He told Hammer he was having a difficult enough time trying to stop smoking ordinary cigarettes, and didn't want the same problem with cannabis.

And he explained to Taffy that he thought his girlfriend would not be too impressed if she thought he had gone to bed with another woman.

Although Hammer and Taffy lived in a kind of semi-criminal limbo, deep down they were vulnerable people who wouldn't have purposely done anyone any real harm.

However, they were not the best of company with whom to get too familiar. Nevertheless, Harry found them interesting, and liked listening to what they had to say about life in Ladbroke Grove. Also Harry's flatmate, Frank, seemed to get some comfort from their "laid back" philosophy on life.

At that time living in this part of London could feel like being on a knife edge. It was the "Teddy Boy" era but you didn't see any Teddy Boys around there, so there was nothing to be concerned about in that respect.

However, every now and then there would be a mention in the KPH that someone had been "bumped off" the previous night in a nearby street.

This never received much publicity, but the policemen would patrol in pairs for the next few nights, just to show they were still in control.

The strange thing was that this did seem to

create a calm environment, and Harry never felt anxious, even when walking back to the flat in the middle of the night.

But the KPH was not far from one of the most notorious streets in London.

This was where the serial killer John Reginald Christie lived at 10 Rillington Place. In 1955 this street was renamed Ruston Close, but after the film "10 Rillington Place" in the early 1970s the whole street was demolished and built over.

It was at this terraced house in Notting Hill that Christie killed at least six women, including his wife Ellen, between 1943 and 1953.

He was also thought to be responsible for the murders of his tenant Beryl Evans and her baby daughter Geraldine. This had originally been blamed on Beryl's husband, Timothy, and he had been charged with her murder.

Christie gave evidence against Timothy Evans at the Old Bailey in 1950, and Evans was found guilty, and hanged.

However, some time later a new tenant at Rillington Place started to discover dead bodies hidden behind walls. Christie therefore arrested, and tried for murder 22

June 1953 in the same court as Evans had been tried three years earlier.

Christie pleaded insanity, and claimed he had a poor memory of the events. The Jury rejected the plea, and after 85 minutes found him guilty.

On 15 July 1953 he was hanged at Pentonville Prison by Albert Pierrepoint, who had also hanged Evans.

Some years later the investivigative journalist Ludovic Kennedy wrote "10 Rillington Place" which virtually proved that the execution of Timothy Evans in 1950 had been a gross miscarriage of justice.

Eventually this case had a big influence on the decision to abolish the death penalty for murder in the UK.

Before the demolition of Ruston Close (which had been Rillington Place before it was renamed) it had degenerated into an even worse slum than it was in Christie's days. It was considered to be one of the darkest, most evil, and frightening parts in the whole of London.

It was nearly two decades after Christie was hanged when Harry arrived in Notting Hill, but that particular cul-de-sac where Christie had lived still had an awful atmosphere.

Harry's flatmate Frank usually came for a drink with him, but he was often short of funds. He had a good degree in literature from Birmingham University, but this hadn't helped him to land a well paid job.

Frank had resorted to working as a "bread loader" at Lyons' bakery in Hammersmith. He did well, in that after two weeks he was promoted to "foreman bread loader", but this was still very low paid work.

He did economise where possible, and often managed to travel free on the Underground. He always had a pocket full of tickets for the Notting Hill Gate destination, and somehow this enabled him to exit the tube station without paying the fare.

Also, his girlfriend knitted him jumpers, which he sold to Harry, on the understanding that he would buy them back when he could afford it. However this approach resulted in Harry having a collection of quite a few nice woolly jumpers.

Once Frank was so short of money he wasn't able to have his shoes repaired, so he resorted to wrapping beer mats in cellophane paper, and placing them in his shoes to protect his feet.

Harry continued working in the boardroom at the bank, wading through the bad debts' reports. After a short while a telephone call was received from his Father, and he was asked if he would like to use the phone in the boardroom to call him back.

He quickly remembered that the final exam results were due out that day, and this must be what his Dad was calling about.

He said that as it was a private matter, he would make the call from one of the public phone boxes across the road from the bank.

As soon as he was in the phone box he became very anxious.

He made the call to his Dad, who confirmed that the results had in fact arrived that morning, and he had "done OK". Harry asked what exactly he meant by that, because he knew that doing OK was not good enough.

It transpired that "doing OK" was his Dad's little joke!

When he was asked to clarify, he said he was very pleased to report that Harry had passed the exams, and was now a Chartered

Accountant.

He went back into the boardroom in the office smiling like a Cheshire cat, and everyone gave him their heartiest congratulations.

Tim, a young man from Australia working on the audit, was sitting next to Harry. He had also just received his final exam results. Unfortunately he had failed, but he was quite philosophical about it, and said he hadn't expected to pass anyway.

Tim said he was going to the OVC (Overseas Visitors Club) in Earls Court to drown his sorrows, and invited Harry to join him so he could celebrate.

Under the circumstances, Harry thought this was an extremely magnanimous offer, and accompanied him to the club.

Tim was a heavy smoker, and during the evening Harry accepted a cigarette from him, and had a smoke. This was not a wise move. The first thing he did the next morning was to go out and buy a packet of cigarettes. It was a very long time before he managed to stop smoking again.

It was on this night at the OVC that Harry met Bobby, a cheerful and vivacious brunette with a good sense of humour. She was to become his girlfriend.

Harry asked her for a dance and invited her to meet Tim.

They all had a few drinks together, before Harry took her to Charing Cross station to catch her train back to Bexleyheath in South East London.

Also, he arranged to see her at Charing Cross station the following Friday evening for a drink after work.

As Harry was working in Gracechurch Street in the City, he decided to walk to the West End to get some fresh air before meeting Bobby at eight o'clock.

After leaving the office he strolled along Cannon Street, past St. Paul's Cathedral, down Ludgate Hill, up Fleet Street and past the Law Courts, then by Somerset House, and into the Strand.

This helped him to get over the cobwebs of the day's audit, and have a couple of pints of Guinness in one of the old pubs which used to be in the side alleys off the Strand. These pubs have now all been demolished, and even in the 1960s they were run down and neglected, but served very good Guinness.

When he met Bobby off the train they walked through Trafalgar Square to a cosy little pub in "theatre land", in a side street just off the Charing Cross Road.

They had a very pleasant evening and got to know each other over a few drinks.

These dates then became quite regular, usually meeting in the same place and going to the same pub.

Sometimes they met at the weekend. On these occasions, rather than take the Circle Line to Charing Cross tube station (now re-named Embankment), Harry would walk from Notting Hill, through Kensington Gardens, Hyde Park, Green Park, and St. James' Park, and then across Trafalgar Square to meet the train. He loved the walks through these London parks, away from the roads and the noise of the traffic. Walking also saved the cost of the tube fare.

Bobby loved the romantic and seductive feel of the Notting Hill district, and liked to visit Harry and the other boys in their flat in Basset Road.

She also invited him to some good weekend

parties in Bexleyheath, but he felt more at home when he got back to London.

Soon it was clear Harry and Bobby were a lot more than just friends, and their caring relationship influenced Harry's choice of music.

Susan Maughan's most famous and successful recording, "Bobby's Girl", got all the way to number three in the UK hit parade in 1962. It soon became Harry's favourite record on the juke box at the KPH, particularly when he learned that Susan was also from the north east of England. (She was born in Concett in County Durham, in July 1942, about ten miles from Bishop Auckland where Harry grew up).

This was a happy and interesting time for Harry, but he knew he needed to do something about changing his job, and find work which was more meaningful and stimulating.

As there was always a big demand in the City for recently qualified Chartered Accountants, he was confident he would soon find an appropriate position.

16

THE ENTREPRENEURS

To achieve his next objective, Harry arranged a meeting with a consultancy which specialised in placing qualified Chartered Accountants in the right kind of job.

He told them that he would like to work for a firm which did the audits and accounts for self-made entrepreneurs.

They arranged an interview for him with a chartered accountant partnership with offices in a street just off the north end of Tottenham Court Road.

This was a Jewish company, and it proved to have exactly the sort of clients that Harry had described.

Their audits were mostly successful businesses run by Jewish families.

They had a number of clients in the East End

of London, and Harry was soon working on the accounts of Archie Shine (Furniture Manufacturer) who had a factory in Clapton.

Mr Shine always had a big cigar in his mouth, and turned up to his office in his pale blue suit which matched his pale blue Rolls-Royce. He would then put on a dust coat over his suit and join his employees working on the benches making furniture. He was a charismatic, larger than life character, who was liked and respected by his employees.

Mr Shine always had a big cigar in his mouth, and turned up to his office in his pale blue suit which matched his pale blue Rolls-Royce

Harry spent quite a lot of time in that part of London, because there were a number of clients in the rag trade, who also had their factories in the East End.

However, he did work in other places.

One job he liked was the audit of a hat manufacturer with a business in Luton. The proprietor was a very pleasant and friendly gentleman. He always made sure there was a nice coal fire burning in the office allocated to Harry for the audit work, and at regular intervals an employee would appear with a tray of tea and biscuits.

The factory was still manufacturing black bowler hats, but the demand for this sort of dress was in decline, with the City gents beginning to adopt a less formal dress. It was a sad development for this business, which had been well run for generations and deserved to continue to succeed.

It was an easy job because the books of account were kept in an immaculate condition.

At another time he worked with a fellow employee, a qualified accountant called Moses, on the audit of an insurance company with offices in Holborn.

This was not a very respectable insurance company. It was quite efficient in processing the insurance premium income and getting it paid into the bank, but the claims handling received very little attention, and they were slow in making payments.

It transpired that the business was soon declared insolvent, but in the meantime it had probably been used as a "cash cow" to finance the other enterprises owned by the proprietors.

Although Moses was a very heavy smoker, Harry admired his self discipline, because he didn't smoke at all on the Jewish Sabbath.

It was coming up to Christmas when they were on this job, and the sun set about four o'clock on the Friday afternoon. This was the start of the Jewish Sabbath, the time when Moses always stopped smoking, and he wouldn't have another cigarette until after the sun set the following day.

One Friday, when they had finished work in the office, they decided to go out for an evening meal. Harry suggested the "Four Aces" restaurant which was in an alley off Carnaby Street.

On leaving the office they jumped on a bus

going in that direction. Moses went straight upstairs, and down to the front, but didn't find an empty seat. Harry was following and saw there were two vacant seats in the stair-well at the rear of the bus. He called out "MOSES" to draw attention to these seats. This alarmed the other passengers and they all turned round with quizzical expressions on their faces. It appeared they thought they were about to have an apocalyptic religious experience.

In the restaurant they ordered steaks, but when they were half way through eating them, Moses pointed out that it was Friday. He knew Harry had been brought up as a Catholic, and at that time Catholics were not supposed to eat meat on Fridays.

Harry wasn't going to waste the rest of his steak and finished eating it. He wasn't concerned about little rules like "not eating meat on Fridays", but as an orthodox Jew, Moses seemed to find this difficult to understand.

*Harry called out "Moses" to call his attention to the
seats in the stairwell at the back of the bus.*

Harry got on well with Moses who was like a gentle, giant teddy bear. He was an unassuming and peaceful man, and Harry got the impression that he probably came from a fairly conservative orthodox Jewish family.

Although Moses was quiet and unassuming, he knew how to enjoy himself. That night he and Harry had quite a lot to drink, and by the end of the evening Harry was a bit drunk, but Moses, who had also had a lot to drink, was still as steady as a rock.

Harry was relieved when he got off the tube at Notting Hill, after having first of all mistakenly taken a train in the opposite direction.

It was at about that time that Bobby told Harry she had been accepted for a job as a nanny to the children of an aristocratic Italian family, and she was going to live with them in Italy. This came as a shock. He was now very fond of her, and said he would visit her in Italy for a holiday.

The family had an annual routine, spending the winter at their home in Rome, and the summer at their other place in Cortina d'Ampezzo, in the Dolomites in the north of Italy.

It was Harry's intention to visit Bobby the following summer.

Meanwhile, after Bobby had gone off to live in Italy, Harry began to feel quite lonely.

They wrote to each other regularly, and usually replied by return of post. He stuck her Italian postcards on his bedroom wall, and these were soon decorating the whole bedroom.

Eventually, some months later they were to spend a memorable summer holiday together in Cortina.

In London, the nights were closing in, and it would soon be Christmas, but London and the UK were about to receive an almighty shock.

This was the winter of 1962/63, and one morning Harry woke up to find a thick blanket of snow outside.

Two feet of snow caused chaos in London, and the mayhem lasted for two months, with average temperatures staying around minus six degrees centigrade.

The first four inches of snow arrived on Boxing Day as Brenda Lee was "Rockin' Around the Christmas Tree" on the wireless.

Then on the night of 29 December, bitter Siberian easterly winds delivered another ten inches of drifting powdery snow.

This was the worst winter of the twentieth century, and the river Thames froze over at Windsor.

To try to keep warm, Harry and his flatmates resorted to spending time in Henneky's pub on the corner of Portobello Road, and Westbourne Grove, where there were two large, roaring log fires.

It must have been about this time when Harry began to formulate plans in the back of his mind to try to spend some future winters in warmer climates.

However it transpired that his first audit, in January in the New Year, was an ice cream factory in Southend. At first he just laughed because he thought they were having a joke. But they were serious, and going to Southend really was like visiting Siberia....it was so bleak, and by far the coldest situation he had ever experienced.

Working for the Jewish firm of chartered accountants had been an unforgettable and very enjoyable experience. He had met some lovely characters, like Moses, and the charismatic Archie Shine, but he now thought it was time to move on.

A consultancy arranged for him to have an interview with Hooper Brothers, one of the big five accountancy firms, with their head office in Gutter Lane in the City, near St Paul's cathedral.

He was pleased when he was accepted for this job because, being one of the top firms, working there would be good for his CV, and with their international connections there would be opportunities to travel.

He soon settled into this new role which was a lot different from his previous jobs. In particular, when working on audits away from London, he appreciated the first class hotel accommodation provided by his employer.

Their head office had a notice board which gave particulars of internal vacancies to alert existing employees to these opportunities.

One day Harry saw a requirement for someone, to be seconded for six months, to work in a place called Mwanza in Tanganyika in East Africa.

When he went home that night he tried to find Mwanza on an atlas. After some time he saw that it was near the Equator, and on the south side of Lake Victoria.

Still with vivid memories of the 1962/63 winter, he decided to apply for this job, knowing that if he was accepted he would be spending the next winter in a very warm climate.

He was appointed to the position, and immediately commenced preparations for his move to East Africa.

END OF PART THREE

Part Four

Assignment in Africa

For Mark and Rachael

With Lots of Love from Dad

Mark and Rachael on Mark's First Day at School in England after returning from living in Bermuda in 1974

17

LEAVING FOR TANGANYIKA

When Harry was accepted for the Tanganyika assignment the first thing he was told was that he would need to be able to drive a car.

This presented him with a problem because he had never driven or even taken a driving test.

He explained this to the Hooper Brothers partners in London, and suggested to them that he could take one month's unpaid leave and use part of that time to take a crash course in driving lessons with the intention of sitting the driving test at the end of the month.

Hooper Brothers agreed to this plan of action but Harry realised he was taking a risk because there was no guarantee he would pass the test at the first attempt...if he failed there could be unacceptable disruption to his planned travel arrangements.

However there appeared to be no alternative because he had already made the commitment to accept the job in East Africa.

He decided to use the time before his departure to tidy up his affairs in the North East, and at the same time take driving lessons, followed by the driving test, in his home town of Bishop Auckland.

He told Frank and his other friends in the London flat that this was his plan, and he would have a farewell drink with them on his return to London before catching his flight to Tanganyika.

When he arrived back in Bishop Auckland his Dad and Mam were pleased to see him but said they couldn't understand why he had decided to go to Africa. This didn't surprise Harry because he was also beginning to wonder why he had made such a big decision, virtually on the spur of the moment.

However on reflection he realised he would be well paid, gain experience, and save some money, which was something that seemed almost impossible living in London.

He thought that when he returned he would

be able to use part of his savings to buy himself a car. This was something he had always wanted to do, knowing it must be easier to get girlfriends when having a car. He also realised that on his return flight from Tanganyika he would be able to stop off in Rome, and have a holiday there with his girlfriend, Bobby.

Harry contacted a driving school in Bishop Auckland and told them he needed to pass a driving test before leaving the UK to live in Africa. They made the reservations and said they would try to make sure he could drive before he left the UK, but they couldn't, of course, guarantee success.

He took his driving lessons seriously, and when it came to the day of the test Harry was quite confident. Fortunately, he passed, but he thought his tutor may have mentioned to the examiner that he needed to drive in Africa. He thanked his instructor for the tuition and for his patience.

Harry was told it was a good idea to apply for an "international driving license" and this proved to be good advice, particularly when he was required to produce it when stopping off in Rome on returning to the UK.

The license was a large and impressive

document with a photo, and information printed in numerous languages including some that looked like Chinese.

In Rome the Italian traffic cops helped Harry to move on when he got into difficulty driving on a busy street, and they asked to see his driving license.

They had never seen anything quite like his international license. Their first impressions may have been wrong, and rather than being an English clown, they began to think he was someone special, and did everything they could to look after him.

When it was time to return to London, Harry's Dad came to see him off at Bishop Auckland railway station.

His Dad seemed to be fully aware of the potential hazards to be faced by Harry on this assignment. This tended to make the send off quite emotional, and in some respects it was a relief when the train eventually pulled out of the station.

After arriving at King's Cross Harry took the tube to Ladbroke Grove and immediately went round to see his old friends at the flat.

They went out for a drink to say "Hasta la vista", and had an enjoyable night.

They asked him if he was taking anything with him when he went to Africa to remind him of home and the UK. Harry immediately showed them a picture of the Heslop family's cat, Bisto, which he had in the window in the front of his wallet.

Even after many years his friends reminded him of the high regard he then had for his cat.

After saying goodbye to his friends Harry spent a restless night. He was concerned he didn't miss his flight the next day, and he was still wondering what he had let himself in for when he had accepted the African assignment.

Harry immediately showed them a picture of the Heslop family cat, Bisto, which he had in the window in the front of his wallet.

The next day Harry managed to get himself to Heathrow airport in time to catch his flight to Entebbe in Uganda, where he was to change to a small local flight to take him across Lake Victoria to Mwanza in Tanganyika.

His flight from London called at Frankfurt, and then went on to Cairo where it stopped to refuel.

Here the passengers were allowed to disembark and wander around the airport terminal to stretch their legs.

As soon as they left the plane they were ambushed by hoards of Egyptians wanting to sell them trinkets, or simply asking the passengers if they wanted their shoes cleaned.

There was a perfectly blue sky, and the heat was particularly intense. Harry felt he was going to melt on the tarmac. He was very uncomfortable, sticking out like a sore thumb as he was still wearing his City pin-striped suit.

He was relieved to re-board the air conditioned plane for the flight to Entebbe, where he disembarked to make the connection for the flight to Mwanza.

The reception area at Entebbe, which was the airport for the Uganda capital, Kampala, was no more than a hut.

Harry sat there for some time and was puzzled because he didn't see any aircraft either on the ground or in the air.

He began to doubt if there really was an aircraft for the rest of his journey. Then he looked out of the window and saw a small plane, which looked as though it had been tied together with bits of string and elastic bands.

There were only one or two other people at the airport but Harry managed to find one. He asked him if he knew when the Mwanza flight would arrive. The man replied,

"That is it,"

and pointed to the little aeroplane that Harry had just seen.

After a short time a pilot strolled into the hut and asked who was the passenger wanting to go to Mwanza. Harry said,

"You must be looking for me,"

and the pilot proceeded to help him load his suitcases onto the aircraft.

The flight across Lake Victoria to Mwanza was fascinating.

The plane flew at a low altitude, giving a clear view of the little islands in the lake, some apparently uninhabited, but others with neat and tidy small homes built with mud; wisps of smoke escaped through their roofs from the domestic fires.

Harry was met at Mwanza airport by an Asian fellow called Mr Mistery, a Hoopers & Lyndon manager from their Mwanza office. He had been sent to meet Harry to give him a lift into town from the airport.

Although Harry was employed by Hooper Brothers in London, his employers were now Hoopers & Lyndon, the Hoopers' international partnership at that time.

Mistery helped Harry to check into the Mwanza hotel, and showed him where the Hoopers' office was. He said he would see Harry there the next day.

Harry went and had a couple of beers at the hotel bar, and then went to bed; crawling under the mosquito net, he felt completely lost and lonely. Everything seemed strange and alien, but he thought if he could only be lucky enough to fall asleep, he may find it easier to adjust to what seemed like a hostile environment when he woke up the next morning.

There was an African sitting on the floor

outside his bedroom door, and Harry later discovered this man was paid a few pence to act as his guard for the night.

Harry did in fact feel quite frightened, never having experienced a night as black as that in Africa near the Equator.

In this part of the world the sun always rises at 6.00am and sets at 6.00pm, both in the winter and in the summer. When the sun sets it seems to happen very quickly; one minute it is bright daylight, the next it is pitch black.

The local "up country" indigenous Tanganyikans have a 12 hour, rather than a 24 hour clock, so when it is 7.00am they say it is one o'clock, and when it is 6.00pm they say it is 12 o'clock. Apparently, they are not interested in the time during the pitch black nights between 6.00pm and 6.00am.

When Harry woke up the next morning, the first thing he noticed was the mosquito net covering his bed, reminding him where he was; once again he felt lonely and lost. However, with the bright daylight he became more positive than he was the previous night and immediately set about getting ready for his first day in the office.

Before he left the UK, Harry had been

advised that the acceptable dress code for the office was a smart shirt and tie, with white shorts and knee-length white stockings. As he had brought a sufficient supply of these clothes with him, he was able to dress appropriately before leaving the hotel for the short walk to work.

18

MWANZA, TANGANYIKA

It's worth having a look at the twentieth century history of the country to which Harry was seconded. Wikipedia on the Internet has been used to remind me of most of the historical aspects of this narrative.

After the First World War, Tanganyika came under British supervision.

In 1964, the legacy of the British supervision was still apparent. Cars drove on the left-hand side of the road, and the unit of currency was the East African·shilling, which followed the use of the shilling in the UK (where at that time the currency was pounds, shillings and pence).

When Harry went to work there in 1964, he formed the impression that there was a tentative union of the three East African nations: Kenya, Tanganyika and Uganda.

When he was living in Tanganyika, Harry drank Whitecap or Pilsner beer, which were brewed by the East African Breweries company, though Tanzania now has its own separate Tanzanian Brewery Company.

The railway company for these three nations was known as the East African Railways.

For many years there has been a ferry on Lake Victoria named *MV Umoja* (Umoja is the Swahili for unity). However, it appears this union of each of these three East African nations was to gradually fall apart after the countries gained independence.

In 1948, a group of young Africans formed the Tanganyika African Association to protest against colonial policies.

By 1953, the organisation was renamed the Tanganyikan African National Union (TANU) and was led by a young teacher named Julius Nyerere. Its aim became national liberation.

Tanganyika became independent in December 1961.

When there was a revolution in Zanzibar in January 1964, Nyerere gave the island politicians a prominent role in a newly proclaimed United Republic of Tanzania. It resulted in the union of Tanganyika with the island of Zanzibar in April 1964, the name Tanzania being adopted in October 1964.

Tanzania has for the most part managed to remain unassuming and low-key. It has steered clear of the political upheavals that have impacted most of its neighbours.

Nyerere received his higher education in Kampala and the University of Edinburgh. After he returned to Tanganyika he worked as a teacher. In 1954, he helped to form the Tanganyikan African Union.

On independence in 1961, Nyerere was elected Tanganyika's first Prime Minister, and following the declaration of a republic in 1962, its first President.

Nyerere left Tanzania as one of the poorest countries in the world. Nevertheless much progress in areas such as health and education had been achieved, in this respect perhaps similar to Fidel Castro's Cuba.

He won many awards for the promotion of international understanding and peace, including the Gandhi Peace Prize in 1985.

He died of leukaemia in London in 1999.

A major road in Mwanza is named Nyerere Road, and another is called Uhuru Street (Uhuru is the Swahili for "freedom", or in this context, "independence").

Tanzanians are known for their warmth and politeness, the dignity and beauty of their culture, and for their tolerance, with Christians and Muslims living side by side in harmony.

Tanzania is just south of the Equator, and Mwanza is in the north of the country close to the Equator.

The economy depends heavily on agriculture and has important rich deposits of minerals including diamonds and gold. The former have been by far the most important, providing the country with its largest percentage of foreign currency earnings.

The diamonds were discovered by John Williamson in 1940 when he found the largest ever diamond deposit: it was more than four times larger than any of the diamond pipes previously found in South Africa.

In the first ten years Williamson put all the profits back into the mine to make it the most modern plant in the world. He was also determined the local population should benefit from the enormous wealth being generated. He named the new township after the local tribal chief, Mwadui, as a mark of respect.

When the extent of the diamond strike became clear in 1945, Ernest Oppenheim offered Williamson two million pounds sterling for the mine. Even though this was an enormous sum of money at the time, and Williamson himself was penniless, he turned down the offer.

By the 1950s, the mine had a labour force of several thousands.

Williamson closely managed the mine until his death in 1958 at the age of 50.

After Williamson died and the ownership of the mine had passed to his siblings, Williamson Diamonds Limited was bought 50/50 by De Beers and the Tanganyikan government in 1958 for just four million pounds sterling.

Notable stones produced at the mine include a large Williamson pink diamond which was presented to the then Princess Elizabeth and Prince Philip upon their wedding in 1947.

Mwadui, the township which the diamond mine founded, is situated about 100 miles south of Mwanza by dirt road through the bush on the shores of Lake Victoria.

Lake Victoria which is the world's second largest lake was named after Queen Victoria by John Speke, the first European to discover the lake.

Tanzania is also the home of Mount Kilimanjaro, and the magnificent Serengeti wildlife national park, which are both just a few hours' drive across dirt roads from Mwanza.

Tanzania's climate is tropical and coastal areas are hot and humid, whereas the central plateau tends to be dry and arid throughout the year. Harry found Mwanza's largely dry and fairly temperate climate very pleasant.

Swahili is the official language of Tanzania and most of East and Central Africa, and is said to be one of the 12 great languages of the world.

When Harry lived in Tanganyika, his knowledge of Swahili was virtually nonexistent, but he quickly found out how to order a pint of his favourite beer at the ex-pats club:

"Whitecap moja baridi sana bwana (one very cold Whitecap, bwana)".

This was a lager beer which was served refreshingly cold in the Equatorial climate.

Harry's first impressions of Mwanza were not very favourable. There were dusty by-ways and only a few properly paved roads, reminding him of the Wild West towns usually portrayed with tumbleweed blowing down the streets.

Nevertheless, as the weeks and months went by, he was to grow to have a strong affection for the place, and more generally to marvel at the big sky, the magnificent countryside, and the wild beauty of Africa.

Now, 50 years later, when thinking back to his time in Mwanza, he recalled having watery eyes when flying across Lake Victoria for the last time on his return journey to the UK.

He had grown to love this remarkable country.

Also, with the benefit of hindsight, he knew that on several occasions he had been lucky to be able to return home all in one piece.

19

THE OFFICE

Angus MacDonald was the Hoopers & Lyndon partner in their Mwanza office.

He welcomed Harry, and told him he was to be provided with a house and a servant. He said the servant's name was "Mzee" and this was the Swahili word for "old man".

He also said he had asked for Harry to be seconded from London to help with the heavy extra work load involved in accounting for the cotton harvest.

Harry thought it would sound very rude to call the servant "old man". However Angus explained that in Tanganyika "Mzee" is a very honourable name, because Tanganyikans have the greatest possible respect for old people.

Harry then heard that Tanganyika had adopted a cooperative agricultural system for the cotton farmers, and there were about 400 societies in the Cooperative.

Each society sent their harvest accounts to Hoopers in Mwanza, and after these had been audited and agreed the society members received payment for their crops.

The concept of the cooperative movement was a good one, and it appeared to be working well in 1964 when Harry was there.

With the farmers all working as part of the Cooperative, they were able to hire technical expertise which they badly needed but couldn't afford when farming as individuals.

From an accounting point of view this work was all basic stuff, but there was a good team spirit in the office, and Harry got stuck into the job with the other employees.

Angus went on to tell Harry that he would be required to accompany him on safaris to other audits, including Williamson's Diamonds and various gold mines.

He also introduced Harry to the Mwanza Ex-Pats club which was only about 100 yards from the house where he was going to live, and also within a mile of the office.

This was all particularly convenient for Harry,

who didn't yet have a car.

Harry was driven up to the house where he met Mzee, who was to be his housekeeper and servant.

Mzee had been attached to the house ever since Hoopers acquired it, and also before that when it was used to accommodate officers from the British Army.

Mzee was a charming old man, slim built, not tall, dressed in a white gown and little flat circular white hat; white teeth shone out of the big smile on his happy black face.

He had been provided with a little brick-built cottage at the bottom of the garden, but he didn't use it because he preferred to walk the five miles back to his village at night.

During the following months Harry grew to have a great respect and admiration for Mzee. Every morning he looked forward to hearing the knock on his bedroom door, and Mzee's announcement,

"Seven o'clock Bwana."

This was the time Harry got out of bed to go to the office.

Although it was one o'clock in "up country" Tanganyika time, Mzee had been trained by the British officers to express this hour in the normal way.

When Harry had guests, Mzee prepared his East African curry speciality. The housekeeper was delighted every time the diners cheered as he brought in yet another little bowl of chopped banana, coconut, and other garnishing.

It was a very pleasant walk from the house to the office in the fresh morning air before the ground was baked by the Equatorial mid-day sun. Nevertheless occasionally it was a bit alarming to see a snake twisting through the dirt to disappear into the grass on the other side of the road.

20

THE "EX-PATS" CLUB

With its spacious and comfortable bar, billiards' room, and tennis courts, the Ex-Pats club was an ideal venue for Harry's leisure time.

He went most nights for a few drinks and a game of snooker, and played tennis there at the weekends.

There were always a few characters sitting at the bar taking in the latest news and gossip.

Some of the members were hard drinkers —— they would go on "benders" for two or three days without going home to bed. Harry often saw them still sitting on the same bar stools they had occupied since the previous night.

Occasionally they would call home and ask their servants to deliver dinner to the club.

When the meals were served they were already

so drunk they thought they had returned to their homes, and would invite their guests to move from their lounge to what they thought was their dining room. Actually all they were doing was moving from where they were sitting to another part of the club bar.

One day Hamish MacTavish, a large soft mineral drinks company's (heavy drinking) regional engineer, was included with Harry as part of a group to attend a drinks party. This was at a home with a semi-circular "in and out" driveway, and a hedge across the front of the garden.

After the drinks, the engineer appeared to be drunk. Nevertheless, he was helped into his car and turned on the ignition.

The car then steered very slowly out of the drive and continued on the same trajectory in a circular movement until it came slowly back, directly through the middle of the garden's front hedge, where it became marooned in the middle of the lawn with Hamish asleep at the wheel.

He was carried off to bed, but it took a couple of days to recover his car from the garden.

Clearly, some of these ex-pats were not the UK's best overseas ambassadors, and their behaviour could partly explain Tanganyika's euphoria when the country was granted independence.

The club had a cat, which hid behind bottles of drink at the back of the bar. When Harry went there for evening drinks he practised his Swahili with the African barman:

"Jambo bwana, habari a casi?" ("Hello master, how is your work going?")

The bar steward would then reply in Swahili, usually saying he was having a good day.

Then Harry would ask,

"Wapi paka?" ("Where is the cat?")

The barman then turned round and immediately tried to spot the location of the cat.

If he got it right, Harry would pay him one penny, otherwise he had to pay a penny to Harry.

The steward seemed to like this game, or on the other hand he might have thought it best to humour Harry in case he wasn't quite right in the head.

When Harry was sitting in the bar at the Ex-Pats club he often thought of his parents' home in Bishop Auckland in County Durham in the North East of England, and the cat behind the bar in the club reminded him of another cat the Heslop family had at home.

This family cat was a lovely friendly and clever animal with a great personality. She was strong and healthy with beautiful, shiny, grey fur. She was called Scaramouche, Scara for short, because she was always up to some mischief.

But this also brought back a very sad memory.

When Harry was five years old and his brother Trevor was six, Mam was frantically packing the cases to get ready for the annual family holiday in Devon, when she noticed there seemed to be something wrong with Scara. The cat had a lump on the side of its head. Mam was too busy to take the cat to Mr Wilson, the vet, so she asked Harry and Trevor to go.

Scara was put in a holdall with a zip on the top and two big handles. Harry held one handle and Trevor held the other one as they walked on their way to the vet. They kept the zip partly open so the cat could put its head out to get some fresh air, and also be able to see where they were going. Scara thought this was great fun and kept poking her head out all the way down to the vets. When they got there they sat in the waiting room, and Harry took Scara out of the holdall and kept her sitting on his knee and stroked her to keep her calm and happy.

When it came to their turn Mr Wilson was very kind and smiled at the two boys and the cat, but when he examined the lump he said he would go into the next room to phone Mrs Heslop to explain what needed to be done. After the phone call he came back and told Harry and Trevor that he would need to keep Scara to see if she would respond to treatment. Harry and Trevor thought this sounded like bad news, but they thanked Mr Wilson and then made their way back home carrying the empty holdall. They were very quiet and didn't talk until they got back to their house.

The next day Mam told them the vet had diagnosed Scara with a bad illness and she had agreed that Scara should be put to sleep. She said Scara had gone to Heaven.

This was an awful experience for the two boys, and it left a scar on their hearts for the rest of their lives.

They loved Scara, and had always looked after her. They couldn't understand why she would never be coming back.

Harry with his brother Trevor taking Scara the cat to the vet.

When Harry set out to go to the club, he always left his porch light on to help when he returned home in the pitch black African night.

He often lost his way along the narrow winding dirt path, and finished up in a nervous cold sweat as he made a beeline through to his front door as he often saw snakes sliding into the grass when on his way to the office in the mornings.

One night, when Harry was setting out for the club, it was so dark he had to return to the house to pick up a torch to guide him back out through the front porch.

Suddenly, a large animal leapt over his shoulder and landed on the ground just in front of him with a heavy thump before running off into the bush.

It had been a hyena Harry had inadvertently trapped at the back of the porch when returning to the house to look for the torch.

This could have been nasty because although hyenas are cowards and usually only hunt in packs, they are very unpredictable when cornered —— it is thought they have the strongest jaws of all animals. Also his neighbour's pet dog had recently been lost, and they said it had been taken by hyenas.

Whoever christened these creatures "laughing hyenas" had an odd sense of humour. The sounds they make are a far stretch from "laughing"; it sounds more like something from the bowels of hell.

One Sunday when Harry was playing tennis at the club, he noticed a young lady sitting on a nearby wall, watching the game. She was attractive with dark brown eyes, jet black hair and an olive complexion, and appeared very confident as she sat there all tucked in, very relaxed and comfortable, like a cat.

After the game she introduced herself as "Peggy" with the "American Peace Corps".

She said she had started watching the tennis on Sundays a few weeks ago, and it had become part of her weekend leisure time. She mentioned she particularly liked it when Harry's tennis shorts crept up his leg when he was serving, because this "turned her on".

Harry thought this must be one of the ways American girls introduce themselves when they first meet a boy.

Peggy was vivacious with a great sense of humour. She became Harry's friend, and later, at the tail end of his time in Africa, his girlfriend.

Harry had never heard of the "American Peace Corps" but never thought to ask Peggy what it was all about. However, it didn't seem to be a very demanding occupation because she appeared to have plenty of free time.

After he left Tanganyika, Harry learned the "American Peace Corps" was created by President Kennedy as a way for Americans to devote time to increasing world peace through volunteer work in developing countries.

Harry thought this sounded a bit like bullshit. There seemed to be a lot of bullshit in America. However he liked the down to earth approach of the New Yorkers, but thought they tended to use an excessive amount of bad language. In fact foul language appeared to be part of the CV required to qualify as a New York cab driver.

At Easter in 1964 Harry and Peggy were joined by another couple when they went on safari to Nairobi for the weekend.

It was on this trip they took their photos sitting on the line on the road which marked the exact location of the Equator.

Easter 1964 also coincided with the first BOAC VC10 aircraft "certification" test flight to Nairobi. This plane was designed for the short runways in Africa, but it also became known as the fastest aircraft for transatlantic flights, and was very popular with passengers and crew.

Barclays Bank seemed to be well established in East Africa and Harry made friends with their Mwanza branch manager, Joe Palermo, who was also a member of the Ex-Pats club.

Joe was a lively character, always arranging tennis and snooker competitions and inventive outings like a picnic on one of the uninhabited islands in Lake Victoria.

He gave instructions for the picnic food to be delivered to the lake's shore, where he had hired local Tanganyikans to row the party to the island. It was a bit spooky climbing ashore on the island, not knowing what to expect. They had to avoid too much exposure to the water in the lake because it could inflict bilharzia, a parasitic flat-worm found in the blood and bladder of residents in the tropics; it causes something like a form of sleeping sickness.

Joe Palermo had hired local Tanganyikans to row the boat to the island.

Harry had been told to be careful with his health while living in the tropics. He took the daily quinine tablet to prevent malaria, and also used salt tablets to recover from the heavy sweating he experienced playing tennis.

When Joe Palermo went on home leave, he loaned Harry his car. It was a Peugeot 203, a medium-sized car produced by the French manufacturer between 1948 and 1960. This was one of the original models, with a very small rear window which reminded Harry of the cars used by Al Capone in the American prohibition gangster films.

It transpired that this car gave Harry one of his most anxious experiences.

He was driving along a narrow, winding dirt road high up on a ridge when he tried to use the foot brake, but got no response...the brake was not working! He then applied the hand brake and managed to slow the car down. At that point he should have abandoned the car, but he thought he had better try get it back home.

By this time Harry's nerves were on edge, and he was sweating profusely. Fortunately, the vehicle had a very robust hand brake which he used to try to control the speed on the steep road.

On two occasions he felt sure he was going to go over the edge into the steep ravine but somehow he managed to get the car home. He never used that car again.

Joe Palermo had failed to mention the car had a problem in that its brake fluid was leaking!

21

SAFARI

The word safari evokes images of men crawling through the bush hunting game, but it is simply the Swahili word for journey; not one particular kind of journey, but any journey, whether by land, sea, or air.

Harry went on safaris for both business and leisure.

One business safari was for the audit of a gold mine near Bukoba on the west shore of Lake Victoria. He was to assist Angus MacDonald, the Hooper's Mwanza partner.

They flew together, and were accommodated at the home of the gold mine's managing director.

The plane they flew in was the same type as the one that had picked Harry up in Entebbe on his arrival from the UK; the one he thought looked as though it had been tied together with elastic bands and bits of string. He had since learned that this particular make of aircraft had one of the best safety records of any in the world.

This audit proved to be quite an eye opener in that it disclosed the mine's chief accountant as an embezzler.

This had to be handled diplomatically in the close knit mining community, and the best way forward was carefully considered with the mine's managing director, who discussed the problem with his London head office.

The accountant's employment with the mine was quietly terminated.

It was clear that this was a mine that had seen better times.

The club house had a bar that must have been about 30 yards long, but there were very few customers.

When someone ordered a drink, the barman, who appeared to be covered in dust and cobwebs through lack of activity, slid the bottle along the bar to the customer like in a Western movie.

At the end of the audit Angus and Harry were

accompanied to the airstrip by security guards to protect the one rather small bar of gold to be flown out on the same plane to Mwanza.

Just before they had left for the airstrip there had been a tropical downpour, and when the plane landed it immediately disappeared behind a huge spray of water from the field.

In view of this severely waterlogged airfield, when the pilot emerged Angus and Harry asked him if he was planning to take off for the return journey, and he said,

"I can give it a go."

This was not reassuring.

The pilot's appearance didn't inspire them with much confidence. He was like a peculiar version of the automatic pilot in the film "Airport".

He was a short arsed little fellow with a squint in his left eye, and a large round head, bald on top but with bright red spiky hair sticking out of the sides partly covering his very large sticky out ears.

There were about four inches of water on the field, which could easily have prevented the plane from getting off the ground. This was in 1964 when it was still thought the 1958

Manchester United Munich air disaster had been caused by ice on the wings. However, in 1968 it was virtually proved that four inches of slush on the far end of the runway had prevented the aircraft from getting off the ground, causing the crash.

It was therefore with some trepidation that Harry and Angus sat in the little aircraft as it revved up and went splashing along the field with water spray blanking out any view from the plane's windows.

The pilot and his precious cargo failed to get into the air at the first attempt, so he taxied back to the starting point and said he would have another go.

Much to everyone's relief on the second attempt he got the plane off the ground, and flew safely back to Mwanza where Angus and Harry accepted his offer of a lift into town.

It was only then that they thought the pilot may have been a bit unbalanced, as he drove his car like a bat out of hell through the livestock in the little African villages, scattering the chickens and goats by the sides of the road.

The next audit was the big one — Williamson Diamonds, where they were treated like royalty. A chauffeur driven car picked them up in Mwanza and took them to the mine, where they were greeted by the managing director and given the use of a luxurious boardroom.

This was when Williamson Diamonds was operating at the peak of its success, with record levels of diamond production. The facilities for the employees were first class, with a golf course, swimming pool, tennis and squash courts, billiard rooms, etc.

Angus and Harry also enjoyed the mine's excellent dining facilities and hotel accommodation, and at the end of the audit the chauffeur drove them over the 100 miles of dirt road back to Mwanza.

A few weeks later, Harry and Peggy and a couple of friends decided to go on safari to spend Easter weekend in Nairobi.

It was on this journey that they took their photos on the Equator where the road passed from the Southern into the Northern Hemisphere.

Harry and Peggy on the Equator where the road passed from the Southern to the Northern Hemisphere

They had a lovely hotel in Nairobi, and the weather was perfect.

Although Nairobi is very close to the Equator, it is very high up, giving it a cool and refreshing climate...perfect for tennis, followed by a round of golf.

The following week Harry took himself for a drive along the dirt roads out of Mwanza, and went a lot further than he had originally intended. It had been a hot day, and it was late afternoon when he decided that he had better turn back home.

It was on the return journey that he fell asleep at the wheel, and was only woken by the car bumping over the scrubland.

When he looked out of the car window he couldn't see the road he had been travelling along. He noted the direction of the car's position, and guessed approximately where he must have left the road, so he decided to drive that way in the hope that he would eventually get back on track.

Fortunately he found the road, but then had to guess the way to Mwanza. It could only be in one of two directions but he had no way of knowing which was the right way, until after driving for about another hour he recognised the outskirts of Mwanza. Luckily he chose the correct direction.

Later that month Harry and Peggy had an interesting outing to the Serengeti National Park. There are notices at the entrance to the park warning visitors that, to avoid attacks from the wild animals, they must always stay in their car and keep the car windows closed.

After driving for some time, past lions and crocodiles, Harry was bursting for a pee.

He drove a bit further on and saw a tree about 20 yards from the dirt road, and he decided to risk leaving the car to have a pee behind the tree.

While he was relieving himself he heard a big thump on the ground just behind him, and there was a creature that looked like a six-foot-long crocodile.

It gave him such a fright he nearly did more than a pee where he was standing.

He was very relieved when the creature ran off. Harry thought it looked like a prehistoric monster...it was, in fact, just an iguana.

It was now time to leave Mwanza and return to the UK, and Harry was looking forward to stopping off in Rome for a holiday with

Bobby.

However, a phone call came through from a partner at Hooper's London head office, and a very posh voice said,

"Ah Heslop, how are you? OK, we hope? We need a body in Khartoum...would you stop off there on your way back to the UK?"

Harry said he was sorry but he wouldn't be able to do that because he already had prior arrangements. Fortunately Hooper's agreed they would need to find some other "body" to do the job in Khartoum.

Harry wanted to show his appreciation to Mzee before he left. He went out and bought him a watch and had it engraved with,

"Asante sana Mzee" ("Thank you very much Mzee").

When he gave it to Mzee, his face dropped and he was clearly disappointed...the last thing Mzee needed was a watch; he could tell the time by the position of the sun during the day, and he didn't bother with a clock at night.

Buying this watch for Mzee was very foolish, and was to be a source of embarrassment to Harry for the next 50 years.

After arriving in Rome, Harry was still

haunted by car brake problems.

Bobby had hired a car for the holiday, but when Harry was driving up a steep hill in heavy traffic towards a crossroads manned by a policeman, he discovered the hand brake didn't work.

As there was a car right up tight behind him, he needed both feet to balance the clutch and the accelerator, so he asked Bobby to stretch across and put her foot on the footbrake.

They were in this position when the gesticulating Italian policeman came to find out what was holding up all the traffic.

This was when Harry's international driving license came to the rescue...the policeman seemed to find it very impressive and proceeded to give Harry and Bobby royal attention, and told all the other irate drivers to calm down and stop blowing their horns.

After a lovely holiday in Rome with Bobby, Harry returned to the UK.

As the years went by, Harry's thoughts often returned to his time in Africa, but in particular to the unforgettable Mzee.

Mzee had very few possessions, but was happy and content.

He had to work hard but was always cheerful.

His warmth and politeness reflected the dignity and beauty of Tanganyika's culture.

He appreciated the local environment as though it was his own little piece of the world.

He didn't worry; leaving the future to the will of God.

He was indeed a truly special and admirable "old man".

End of Part Four

& End of Book One

About The Author

Michael Parfitt was born in 1939 in the North East of England where he grew up.

He now lives near London in Surrey with his wife, Anne.

His family, including two grandsons, all live nearby in London and in Surrey.

Michael qualified as a Chartered Accountant in April 1962, since when he has been a fellow of the Institute of Chartered Accountants in England and Wales.

He has always been a supporter of Sunderland AFC.

Arry Eslop is Michael's first book. It is the

biography of an imaginary person who grew up in the North East of England about 70 years ago.

Michael will be pleased to receive any comments on this book. Please forward your views to his email address:

sunderlandmike@hotmail.co.uk

Paperback copies and a Kindle version of this book are exclusively available on the Amazon website.

19549294R00118

Printed in Great Britain
by Amazon